PENGUIN BOOKS

Over Our Heads

'The stories are wonderfully crafted and cared-for, the undertones are witty and ironic, but also serious and filled with sympathy' Colm Tóibín, *Guardian*

'*Over Our Heads* is full of surprises, all of them great' Roddy Doyle

'Deft, clever, intense – this is a terrific debut from a very gifted new writer' Kevin Barry

'Andrew Fox's stories are slivers of power; knowing, watchful and burning with intelligence. Lives half-lived or grasped at; loves longed for and destroyed; the journey of the modern emigrant who goes away in the same daze in which he comes home: these are stories which linger long after they have been read' Belinda McKeon

'Fox is skillful at probing the bigger emotions: alienation, loss and nostalgia. His sparse prose is an effective counterpoint to complex feelings. His stories deal with the moments that shape a life: first trysts, the illness of a parent, the graduation of a child . . . Fox knows the hallmark of a good short story: leave the reader wanting more' *Financial Times*

'An impressive and thoroughly enjoyable collection . . . Fox lets his characters tramp around their worlds, searching for heaven on earth' *Irish Times*

'A remarkable new talent . . . He is able to tread so lightly that we only realize we have been cleverly punched in the solar plexus after we finish the last line' *Irish Mail on Sunday* (five stars)

ABOUT THE AUTHOR

Andrew Fox was born in Dublin in 1985. He now lives in New York. *Over Our Heads* is his first book.

Over Our Heads

Andrew Fox

PENGUIN BOOKS
LEABHARLANN CHONTAE
LIATROMA
LEITRIM COUNTY LIBRARY

PENGUIN BOOKS

UK | USA | Canada | Ireland | Australia
India | New Zealand | South Africa

Penguin Books is part of the Penguin Random House group of companies
whose addresses can be found at global.penguinrandomhouse.com.

Penguin
Random House
UK

First published by Penguin Ireland 2015
Published in Penguin Books 2016
001

Copyright © Andrew Fox, 2015

The moral right of the author has been asserted

The following stories previously appeared, sometimes in
substantially different form, in the following places:
'Pennies' and 'A Vigil' in *New Irish Writing*;
'Manhood' in *Prairie Schooner*;
'The Parcel', 'Everything', 'Graduation' and 'Are You Still There?' in *The Dublin Review*;
'Occupations' in *The Massachusetts Review*;
'A Man Should Be Able to Do Things' in *A Modest Review*;
'Strong' in *The Stinging Fly*;
'How to Go Home' in *Cuadrivio* and on RTÉ Radio 1

Set in 12.65/16.62 pt Perpetua Std
Typeset by Jouve (UK), Milton Keynes
Printed in Great Britain by Clays Ltd, St Ives plc

A CIP catalogue record for this book is available from the British Library

ISBN: 978-0-241-96895-6

For E

Contents

Pennies   1

Manhood   10

The Parcel   22

Stag   40

Two Fires   53

A Vigil   68

Occupations   75

A Man Should Be Able to Do Things   94

Everything   104

Strong   117

How to Go Home   131

The Navigator   139

Graduation   159

Stations   174

Are You Still There?   181

Pennies

My mother had been in secret talks with someone on the phone all week, but it wasn't until she brought out the good tablecloth that I knew I was being set up. She smoothed out the creases, arranged cutlery and plates. And when the doorbell rang, she went to bring him in: a stretched, paler version of the kid from junior school who used to eat his slimy ham sandwiches alone in a corner of the yard. I hadn't thought about Alan in years. I, like everyone else, had forgotten all about him.

His hair and his eyes were colourless, but a fat bruise purpled his cheek. He forked over Mam's grey chicken casserole and mumbled bullshit compliments. We talked in awkward spurts about birthday parties that only my mother remembered. My father, still chewing, left to watch the news in the sitting room. And then, when Alan excused himself to go to the toilet, Mam made tea and laid it on thick with:

'He's really a wonderful boy, you know. I was always very fond of him.'

'Yeah,' I said, watching milk flower in my cup, 'but he's creepy.'

Mam sat beside me, leaning close. Alan's mother, she said, had been having trouble with her nerves for years, even before the divorce and the move away to Dublin. She was staying for a month or two with a sister out in Galway, and had sent Alan back to spend the summer with his father. As my mother spoke, her eyes watched mine, her lips curving in a smile that described to me my own perfection.

'And I'm sure,' she said, 'that being seen with you would do wonders for his street cred.'

Of course, I knew what she was trying to do. But she knew me better.

'That's true,' I said.

My mother. I swear to God, she should have gone into politics.

That summer I was working at the Lifeboat, a pub on the harbour road. The customers there were men from the trawlers, big fellows with cloudy eyes and hard cheeks webbed in veins. Their hands shook as if groping for the salvation the pub's name seemed to offer, though there wasn't one among them who could have been redeemed. I collected their empty glasses, gave them change for cigarettes, listened to their opinions and suspicions and advice. Every day, when my shift ended, I'd need to get out a little frustration.

Alan and I started going to the train tracks to put pennies on the rails. It was something he used to do, he said, when he was younger. The tracks ran towards Dublin on an embankment between small fields. On either side, the embankment fell away to deep gulleys overgrown with bramble bushes. A dirt track ran alongside the rails, and it was this that Alan and I followed. He taught me to put the pennies on the inside edge of an easy curve, so that they'd ping into the safety of the gravel between the sleepers. I imagined that every penny I placed was someone from the pub, or sometimes Alan, or sometimes me. I'd cover my ears as the train roared by, then comb the stones to find them stretched and made anew.

One time, searching for a penny that had flown into the bushes, Alan and I discovered a cleared passage leading down into the gulley's darkness. He edged forward, skidding as the earth slipped, then disappeared. I got down on to my arse and scooted in after him. The descent was steep, studded with rocks and roots. We found ourselves a good ten feet below the level of the tracks, in the mulchy smell of a canopied hollow sunk at the end of a cornfield. A short ridge of piled earth separated the hollow from the field, matted with long grass and strewn with blackening branches.

Alan and I rooted around among the leaves, smoking cigarette ends I'd pocketed from the Lifeboat's ashtrays. We found bits of rusted metal, the broken sides of fish crates, old fertilizer bags, a pair of women's underwear. We opened a plastic shopping bag to find an ancient porno, the image on its cover rain-faded and sun-bleached. The pages were stuck together and all but decomposing. The women were hairy and dead-eyed, and older than our mothers.

We stayed in the hollow for hours, making up stories about the people who had been there long before us. It was clear, Alan said, that they were perverts, and that the country did that to people. Something about the quiet here could twist you up, he said, but you weren't safe in the city either because of all the noise. I asked him about his mother, about his friends, about his school. He asked if I knew Bill Coleman, who he said was the owner of the cornfield. Coleman, Alan's father had said, shot trespassers on his land, and once, when he'd found a dog sniffing around his chicken coop, had levelled his shotgun at the hip and put a bullet through its eye.

Alan never came into the pub, but most days, after work, I'd find him waiting for me in front of the church, or sometimes further up the street if there was a gang outside the chipper. In time, I learned to like him, to find comfort in our routine. His voice was clear, his eyes cold. He knew things about history and politics. He never laughed.

'The child just needs someone,' my mother said over Sunday lunch. 'You're very good to be spending time with him.'

'Just you mind you watch yourself,' my father said as he pushed away his plate.

'But he'll get his reward,' my mother said.

'Oh, so that's how it works?'

One night, Alan called to the house with a bottle he said he'd stolen from his father. He had a fresh bruise I didn't need to ask about, and his breath was shallow. We passed the bottle between our sleeves on the walk out of my estate. We joined the dirt track and followed the line of the rails, our steps unsure in the dark. At the passage, we found the shapes of two girls. I felt Alan tense when he saw them, heard them giggle when they saw us. I couldn't see their faces. Shouts rose from the hollow.

'Come on,' Alan said and dragged me further along.

We left the tracks at the bridge and walked the back roads for hours. We found a half-built cottage and sat on the raw concrete floor of its kitchen to finish the bottle. As the sky began to lighten, I puked through a glassless window.

'I'm taking you home,' Alan said and helped me to my feet.

He led us through the grounds of a ruined church, past the turn for the quarry and in the back way to my estate. In the driveway, he told me to shake his hand. I reached for it but missed. His forearm at my shoulder steadied me.

'I'm coming in with you,' he said.

At the kitchen table, Mam was waiting up, her arched hand poised on fingertips like a snooker player's.

'Is your father home?' she said to Alan.

'I don't know,' he said.

'It's very late,' she said. 'Go on to bed, the both of you.'

We took off our shoes and crept up the stairs, but Dad caught us on the landing on his way back from the toilet. He was wearing his pyjamas, the jiggle of his gut showing where he'd missed a button.

'Let me smell your breath,' he said and took my jaw in a heavy hand.

I blew through rounded lips.

'Jesus Christ,' he said.

Alan's eyes were white.

'Go home,' Dad said to him. 'Right now.'

I crawled into bed and kept a foot on the ground to stop the room from spinning. I heard my door creak open and knew that it was my mother. She stood for a long time, watching me, saying nothing. Then she left and I lay awake listening through the wall to the sound of her fighting my father.

In the morning, Dad read his paper at the table and Mam cooked a big breakfast. I choked down greasy sausages and padded myself with toast. No one spoke as we ate. But before I left for the Lifeboat, Dad told me that I wasn't to see Alan any more.

I looked to my mother.

She stared out the window at her washing filling with wind.

After work, I went looking for Alan outside the church but I couldn't find him. I made my way to the dirt track, and as I walked past the silent blackberry bushes I thought about something he'd said or I'd dreamed he'd said the night before: that soon everything would be different. Closer to the city, fields were being levelled and new apartments were rising. One day our town would grow into the next one over, and like that it would spread, along the commuter line and on into Dublin, just houses and towns all the same place and nowhere to go to escape them. I was sad for Alan thinking that. But for the moment I felt as though I were walking in an old map where the world finds an edge and the sea spills over into nothing.

No one was waiting by the passage. I slid down into the hollow. Alan was sitting on a tree stump trying to roll a penny across the backs of his knuckles.

'I suppose your parents hate me now,' he said.

I stared at the dirt on the toes of his yellowing runners, the baggy drape of his jeans across bony knees. I looked into eyes that needed me, and was embarrassed for us both. All day, the one thing I'd thought about, my arms heavy with glasses or my cheek red from the washer's steam, was getting to Alan, but now all I could think about was getting away from him. Climbing out of the hollow was hard. You had to take long strides on the loose earth and grab for a branch at the top. More than once I'd missed and slid back down on my stomach. More than once my shirt had ridden up and stones dug into my chest.

Alan made a fist around the coin. I looked away from him towards the opening of the passage, a jagged shard of dusky sky where the high leaves shook. Then I saw a flailing hand miss a branch, saw Alan slip and fall. The rails began to sing. He picked himself up and ran again and caught the branch and hung on tightly. His feet scrabbled in the dirt as leaves whipped up around him. The horn grew loud and strong. I realized what was happening.

I dived for Alan's ankle and held on. He kicked me hard in the chin and my vision went black, then red. Black was the train tearing past. Red were the wind and the leaves. Alan finally let go and the two of us rolled back to the bottom. He mumbled something with no breath.

'The hell were you thinking?' I said.

Under a torn flap of denim, Alan's shin was cut and swollen. He reached a hand through the hole and brought it out blood-smeared. We lay together listening to each other's breathing. Darkness fell around us quickly, the way it does beyond street lights.

'We're going,' I said, but I knew I'd leave alone.

I couldn't face the climb so I scrambled over the branches and the ridge and set off across the field. The corn stalks were shoulder-high and the ploughed earth was uneven. I kept one eye on Bill Coleman's farmhouse, black and squat nearby. No light showed in its windows, but I was sure that someone waited. It was quiet but for the breath in my lungs. I ran out of nameless fear. Fourteen is too young to learn that the mind of

God may hold two opposing ideas at once, without ever showing a preference for either.

I made it as far as the road before I looked in guilt for Alan. In the darkness I could see back no more than a few feet but I could hear another train in the distance. Before my eyes, the wind moved the branches of a tree. It joined their leaves together like hands in a moment of silent prayer, then divided them again into something else.

Manhood

The pit lies open before me and Puppy as though ready to swallow the sun. Briars swell behind and around us, and the bank slopes away at our feet. The air here is heavy with the tang of dirt and animals. And down there, where once they quarried ballast for the trawlers, are the lime lines and the goalposts and the shipping containers used for changing-rooms. The team that threw Puppy off for fighting are getting stuffed by some shower from Raheny. He speaks his mind:

'You're a *donkey*, Damo!'

'Big banana feet on you!'

'I've seen *milk* turn quicker!'

This is the life, panned out on the warm grass with a can and the last of the smokes Puppy got from his Da last week. The Big Dog's a trucker, comes home only twice a month.

'Look,' he says and hunches forward, 'check it out.'

This right here is an excitable lad at the best of times, so it could be anything he's pulling from the inside pocket of his jacket. Still, I'm surprised by what he shows me. Of course, I've seen johnnies before.

'What are you carrying that around with you for?'

'To show you, you virgin prick.'

I try to concentrate on the match below, but Puppy won't be stopped.

'You'd think Karen was a quiet one, yeah? Well, I'm here to tell you, son – the noises out of her? My Jesus! Like nothing on earth, she was.' He scratches his eyebrow with the back of a thumb and pauses. 'Listen here.'

'I'm listening.'

'But are you hearing?'

'Despite myself.'

'She has a mate.'

'Has she, now?'

Damo Daley belts one over the bar from the corner and I surprise even myself with the force of the cheer I let out, so keen am I to show my passion for a sport I've never been bothered with.

'The fuck,' Puppy says, 'is your problem?'

'Nothing, just . . . Good point, yeah?'

'Oh, stellar,' he rolls his eyes. 'Christ. Get your yoke working and talk to me, yeah? Boys in shorts and here's you delighted.'

I finish my smoke, grind it into the back of an ant in the wrong place at the wrong time.

'So,' I say. 'Who's the friend, then?'

Puppy sniffs and clears his throat.

'Eits.'

Eits. When we were nine years old and kiss-chasing, Eithne Killeen let everyone catch her. Twelve and playing spin the bottle, she let anyone use the tongue. Fourteen, she was suspended from school for wanking off Mark O'Leary in the boys' jacks at lunchtime. Fifteen, she discovered vodka and ended every party by puking her ring in your living room. She smells like baby powder, bleaches the shite out of her hair, wears thick eyeliner and thin shirts you can see her nipples through. She lives two streets away. Our fathers were friends until Eits' da died. When I was five and starting school she held my hand in the yard. I always nod 'hello' whenever I see her. But she scares the living shit out of me.

Friday night, Puppy has a free gaff. I knock over and he answers the door shirtless, sockless – glowing ginger head on him. He leads the way upstairs towards his bedroom, where he has his stereo set up and where we're allowed to smoke out the window. But when we get to the landing, he pauses, holds a finger to his grinning lips and flings the door open.

'Fuck *sake!*' Karen says and grabs for the edge of the sheet.

I can't really see anything good, but what I can see is almost better. A long slope of rib and side-tit. Dark hair hanging in her face.

'Turn your fucking eyes, yeah?' she says. 'The both of yous.'

We study the *Scarface* poster on the wall, Pacino blasting an M16 in black and white and red. Puppy winks when he catches my eye.

'Okay, right,' Karen says. 'Look, so.'

She wears black jeans and a tight black jumper with fraying sleeves hooked over her thumbs. Her feet are bare, her toenails purple. She pulls her knees to her chest and hugs them. Puppy sits beside her and starts chewing at her neck.

'Karen? Boyo here needs the lowdown on Eits. I've told him she's gagging, isn't that right?'

'Well –'

'There you go,' Puppy says. 'You're on a promise, there. She doesn't lie to her friends.'

'She'd love it if you did,' Karen says.

'If I what?'

'If . . . you know. I think she likes you.'

'If he threw her the good length!' Puppy bounces on the mattress. 'You brought the big knob, yeah?'

Karen smoothes a hank of hair at her ear and fumbles behind her for Puppy's cigarettes. She lights one, looks at the floor.

The sign outside says *Riders Niteclub*. A chunky cowgirl sits astride the belly of the 'd'. Her spurs graze the 'e's kicker. She licks her lips and waves her hat and winks. This is not a classy place.

By now we've all got a bit on us. Me: a shoulder I drained on the harbour road. Karen: just the few snifters of Bacardi she's been sipping from a Coke bottle. Christ knows about Puppy: he's sniffling like a lunatic, licking his lips and chewing his gums. I'm still waiting for results from the yoke he palmed me in the hall.

The bass rumbles low in my chest as I approach the door. Karen lives just around the corner and can get us in for free, but me and Puppy do the sober walk past the bouncers just in case. We leave our coats, get our hands stamped and head through padded doors into thumping techno and epileptic strobe light and throat-clawing dry ice and wet heat. Bodies are everywhere, their smells mixed in the air with the reek of Jägermeister and Red Bull and whiskey and beer and cider. We do quick shots and shove on to the dance floor where Puppy and Karen rub their crotches together. And I bob and weave and stretch and give it socks now because, looking at myself in the mirrored walls and realizing that I am suddenly in love with everyone and that no one could possibly hurt me, I'm coming up pretty strong.

After a while I go to the back bar to catch my breath. 'Whiskey and Coke!' I shout and the bartender nods like, Yes! Here finally is someone who orders a man's beverage.

A girl looks up from a few feet away and raises a glass

coloured with the same drink. I pull a stupid face to make her laugh and she turns to face me and pushes out her chest. I sidle up, yipped to bits and cool as a cucumber. And I'm off:

What's your name? That's a nice name, unusual, exotic. I had a fish called that once. Only buzzing. No, it's nice. Beautiful, yeah? You from around here? Course you are. Why else'd you be in a shithole like this? Stop, sure I know. But it's what we have to work with, right? You play the hand you're dealt, yeah? So, do you go to school around here? Course not. What am I saying? I'd have noticed someone like you. Couldn't miss someone as gorgeous as you. I'm serious! What? You think I'm messing? I'm not messing at all! I wouldn't bullshit you. I'll always tell *you* the truth. Here, you're something else. Really, now, really. So what do you want to be when you grow up? Really, zoology? Never knew anyone who did that before. Animals and shit, yeah? That's cool. I like animals myself – for dinner! Only messing. But that's great, no seriously. It's good you know what you want to do. Me? Just chilling. Like a villain on penicillin, what? Just weighing the options, you know yourself. Yeah. Nah, it's grand. Sure, I'll figure it out. Course I will. Here, here you're gorgeous. You are *gorgeous*! Do you want to dance? Would you like to dance with me? Really? Deadly. I mean, all right if you want to. Whatever. Lead the way . . .

And down to the dance floor we go. She actually takes my hand to guide me through the throng so we won't get separated. We squeeze into the half inch of available space there is behind some lanky streak with sharp elbows and some diddy little looker all giggles and bounce – the weirdest couple in the world. And we're hopping and bopping to the loud fast music on the tight hot dance floor. And I'm trying really hard to hold it together, breathing carefully and riding the crests and the troughs and gumming the face off myself but making sure she doesn't notice, when I catch Puppy's eye and he gives me the wink and a big 'Surprise!' face and licks his lips and grabs two enormous handfuls of Karen's arse.

I look back at my bird and reckon I might just be on to a winner, here. Blondie. Tall. One of those special ones who people give space to and smile at without really knowing why. And true to form there's room clearing around her as she pops those hips and swings that hair and lets it fall wherever. And of course there's pretenders – it's the law of the jungle out here, boys! Lads sidle up and try it on, and I think I might be finished just for a second each time, but she shrugs them all off and turns back to me where I'm scissoring the air in front of me like a maniac – stacking shelves, making boxes, mop that floor, big-fish-little-fish – because I haven't the foggiest notion of what else to do. Sweating like a bastard. Breathing like a train. Chemicals fizzing and popping in my veins . . .

And. Now. Suddenly. I'm on the floor with my ears ringing. I stagger to my feet and blink the spots away from my eyes. And there's my girl, crisp in strobe-light stop-motion, arguing with some monster who can only be her boyfriend. Shaved head. Scarred knuckles. Tricolour tattoo.

She legs it off to the jacks crying – thanks a bunch! – and he comes over to lean his head against mine and shout and spit all over my face. Then he rears back and nuts me on the bridge of the nose. The room explodes around me. When I come to I'm being held up by two bouncers, then being flung through a doorway clear and slow. And now Puppy and Karen are beside me. She kneels down to rub my head and hold a tissue to my nose to stop the bleeding, and her hand feels nice and cold, her breath feels nice and warm, and I almost think I hear myself say 'I love you' but I can't be sure because she doesn't even flinch.

Puppy's been on his phone all the way down the street telling the story. There's drink in the house, he says, but not enough to go around.

'But don't worry,' he tells me, 'I've got you covered.'

He goes to the fridge and comes back with two cans and a bottle of some neon-yellow alcopop. And for a moment I realize I miss like hell the times when it was just the two cans, just the two of us.

'Get that into you, Cynthia,' he says.

The rest follow soon enough: some girls Karen knows from the convent, a few of the boys looking the worse for wear. Mark O'Leary is telling a joke about an octopus. Eits trails in last. Her heels are about seven storeys high and her clothes are tight in the right places. Puppy sits beside me.

'All right, chief,' he says, 'Karen's had a chat and it's all good to go. This is the long and the short of it: you fucked it up with your one in the club, so this is all there is.'

'I didn't fuck it up,' I say, 'I was on a promise there if it wasn't for –'

'You have to. You *have* to. Look, you're a man. But you're not. And you need to be.'

'You're an idiot.'

Puppy throws a glug of his drink down his throat. 'But I'm a man, though.'

Eits and Mark are exchanging words. I manage to catch: '. . . just a little one. Two minutes. I've balls on me like fucking melons.'

'Fuck off, you.'

'Here,' Mark says, 'Puppy, throw us a can there, yeah? And a pint of seawater if you have it for this beast here beside me.'

Eits storms through the double doors to the sitting room.

'Follow her,' Puppy says, his smile toothy and wolfish.

From across the room, Karen nods.

Eits says, 'Do you have a condom?'

One thing has led swiftly to another, and here we are. She's down to her pants, her tits enormous and run all over with pale blue veins. I lie on my back with my shirt off and my jeans and boxers around my ankles. Her mouth tastes like cigarettes.

'No,' I tell her.

'It's okay. I do.'

She opens her bag and takes out a condom, unwraps the foil with ease and tries and fails to put it on me. One thought does the revolutions around my brain and won't leave me in peace. I'm thinking that neither of us, by a long shot, is the other's first choice.

'What's wrong with you?'

'Nothing.'

'You're nervous?'

'Yeah.'

'And drunk?'

'Very.'

'And yipped?'

'Yeah.'

'Okay.'

Eits throws the condom across the room, takes another from her bag and lays it on the couch beside me.

'Jesus, you've some stock.'

'You never know,' she shrugs. 'Relax.'

And now her chin and her teeth are on my stomach. She must get a hair in her mouth because she sits up gagging and spits.

'Sorry.'

'No problem.'

She goes back. And I can feel her lips on me again. I think of the taste of her breath. I remember her looking after me in school.

'It's not worth it,' she says.

I can hear them all out there in the kitchen. The hush when she enters. And the roars of laughter when the story is told.

I lie in the dark and try to read the titles of Puppy's Ma's CDs, try to ignore the thick smells of old cigarettes and dust rising from the couch. I listen to the others getting drunker, to things breaking. And then I listen to the murmur of someone talking sense into someone else. I listen to the last of the music, to the phone calls and the goodbyes. I hear Puppy race heavily up the stairs, hear Karen say:

'I'll be up in a minute.'

The door opens. I pretend to be asleep. Karen sits on the couch beside me and puts her hand in my hair.

'I'm asleep.'

'Good dreams?'

'What do you think?'

'I can imagine.'

'Am I a laughing stock?'

'Oh, fuck *them*. Don't worry about it.'

I sit up. Karen doesn't move. My arm brushes hers.

'But I do worry about it.'

'I know.'

'Puppy doesn't worry.'

'No,' she laughs. 'He most definitely does not.'

She tosses her hair out of her face. Her eyes are massive and shining and she won't lift them from me.

'You don't like me very much,' she says, 'do you?'

'I like you.'

'You think I'm changing him.'

'I don't.'

'You think I'm stealing him.'

'I did. I don't.'

'Are you skagging?'

'A bit.'

'How's your head?'

'I think I'll live.'

She bends to kiss my forehead. And the way she smells is something I know I'll always save just for me.

'It'll work out.'

'Will it?'

I watch her walk backwards, the blades of street light from between the blinds carving her body into sections. I expect her to turn and leave but she doesn't. She just stands there and watches me for a moment.

And then she comes back.

The Parcel

Some years ago, my girlfriend and I pooled our savings, borrowed a large sum of money and bought an apartment in a new development that had just gone up by the motorway. There were no shops, but lots of ground-floor units whose windows bore 'coming soon' notices alongside pictures of even-complected women holding baskets of smooth fruit. An organic supermarket, the smiling estate agent told us, was in the works. A coffee bar was imminent. A gym was on final approach. The apartment had a two-person bath, a zinc-topped kitchen island, power outlets for plasma TVs fixed halfway up the wall. We decorated it with money and restraint and then sat back and waited for the city to come to us.

By the end of our first year, it had become apparent that it never would. Fewer than half of the postboxes in the lobby had names attached and most of the balconies were conspicuously bare of furniture. One night that winter I rode the lift to the top floor and was confronted with an empty hallway, torn plastic sheeting in lieu of windows and a red EXIT sign flickering in the darkness. Spooked, I dived back into the lift before the doors had closed, and was gripped by a terrible loneliness as I watched the floor numbers blinking down.

Then, last spring, Sarah's company restructured and moved her to London. We skyped each other every night, she jetted back to me on weekends, and I pretended that I was the type of person who could live like that. I didn't tell Sarah that, in her absence, I was eating most of my meals from a single bowl which, when not in use, I kept upturned in the sink; that I was sleeping late, drinking alone, masturbating with unsettling frequency. When she'd phone on Friday evenings to say she'd landed, I'd run a quick hoover over the place, deodorize my tobacco stink, order Indian food. And when she'd get in I'd watch with nervous discomfort as she pottered from room to room.

One Saturday afternoon, I woke alone and was unable to work out why. I lay, blinking at the ceiling, and turned this anomaly over in my mind. Then it came back to me: Sarah was at a conference in Stockholm. I felt guilty at having forgotten to skype her the previous night, until I realized that she too had neglected to skype me. Then I felt wounded. Still in the sweatshirt and tracksuit bottoms I'd slept in, I rode the lift down to the lobby to collect the post from the day before. I opened our postbox and was surprised to find a parcel waiting for me: an amorphous lump, wrapped in brown paper and bound with butcher's twine. I inspected it, and was saddened to find that it had been addressed to Turlough Lannigan in 3E.

Back in the apartment, I turned the parcel over carefully in my hands. I traced the lines of its handwritten address with my fingers and fought the urge to open it. Then, touched by the notion of people, out there, taking the time to wrap things, write things and send things to each other, I went to my computer and found a florist's website, where I selected and paid for a bouquet of tulips and entered the address of Sarah's apartment. It was only when I was outside Turlough Lannigan's door, the sound of my knock echoing in the empty hallway, that I remembered that Sarah would be in Stockholm for most of the week. My mind played a movie of tulip bulbs planted, nourished, germinating, tended to, growing, blooming, harvested, wrapped in cellophane, bound with ribbon, placed in a refrigerated truck and driven through the streets of a foreign city towards a locked door, while the person for whom they were intended got on with her life, hundreds of miles away.

I knocked again, and as I waited I thought of Sarah, missing her more than I could remember ever having done. The door opened and brought me face-to-face with a man and a woman.

'Yeah?' said the man, Turlough.

'Seen a dog?' said the woman, Mrs Turlough.

'I have a package,' I said. 'They left it in the wrong box.'

Turlough took the parcel and looked me over, blinking.

'Kevin,' I said, extending a hand. 'I live downstairs.'

'Maria,' said the woman.

'Turlough,' said Turlough. 'Have you seen a fucking dog?'

'A dog?' I said.

'She's got out,' said Maria.

'No. But do you need a —'

'No.' Turlough straightened his glasses on the bridge of his nose to bring me into sharper focus. 'I can find her. You're grand.'

Maria cocked her head to one side and considered me from an angle. She had narrow, feline eyes, a dimple in the centre of her forehead. She leaned away from Turlough — arms crossed beneath her breasts, feet shoulder-width apart — as though she were trying to build strength into her posture. Turlough leaned towards her, attracted but forewarned. He had done some-thing, I could tell, for which she might never forgive him.

Turlough had one sandalled foot in the hallway. Fronds of waxy hair spiralled from the toes. 'Here,' he said and handed the parcel to Maria. 'I'll go out.'

'All right.' Maria was still frowning at me.

'You stay here in case she comes back.'

'Okay.'

'I'll find her.'

'See that you do.'

Turlough aimed a kiss at Maria's lips but she turned at the last moment and his nose bumped against her ear. He flashed me an uneasy look and left.

'Tea?' Maria said.

I searched for excuses but came up empty. 'Sure,' I shrugged, and stepped into an apartment I found eerily familiar, like the figure of a stranger you might feel compelled to wave at in the street. Their TV was a little bigger than ours, but cheaper. Their stereo was vastly inferior, I was pleased to note. I liked the set-up of the bookshelves, though: they carved the open-plan living area in an interesting way. I admired too the arrangement of the floor lamps: even in daylight I could tell that it would make for superior illumination. But most impressive was the way the place smelled: like soap, perfume and time-intensive cooking. It made me feel guilty about the slide in standards over which I was presiding.

'I'll put the kettle on,' Maria said, rubbing her elbows.

'Grand.'

I walked to the window. Their view was almost the same as ours, except, from this slightly greater height, they could see beyond the graffitied wall of blue construction hoarding that faced our building and truncated my own perspective. I looked out over the waste ground that surrounded the development on three sides. Kids in dirty trainers and warm coats were milling about in the long grass. I wanted to be outside, to breathe the air they breathed.

'I don't understand it,' Maria said over the whistle of the kettle. 'The lock broke yesterday. And he told me he'd fix it and of course he didn't. But that doesn't explain how the dog got out now, does it? Do you follow me? How did she do it?'

'Weird all right.'

'Did she jump up and turn the handle, I'm saying? Does she always do that when we're not here?'

'Right.'

'I mean, anything could happen. When you think about that it's terrifying.'

Maria had left the parcel on the kitchen island. Beside it, she placed two cups into which she dropped tea bags and poured water.

'Lumps?' she said.

'None, thanks.'

'Moo juice?'

'Just a splash.'

She joined me at the window. I took my tea and stood for a moment, envying still the extra sliver of life that they could see and we could not.

'She'll come back,' I said, and the uselessness of the sentiment forced me to say it again.

'She will or she won't,' Maria said with a shrug. 'Sit.' She picked up the parcel and brought it to the couch.

'Are you going to open it?' I eased myself into the leather armchair facing the door.

Maria's fingers traced the lines of the address, as mine had done a short time before. She weighed the parcel, shook it and, with a sad smile, set it down. 'I'd better not. No, it's not addressed to me. It wouldn't be right.'

I made a show of looking around at the apartment. 'Your place is lovely.'

'I'm sure it's pretty much the same as yours.'

'It is and it isn't, if you know what I mean. We should have you two down, though. To see, like. Sometime.'

'That'd be nice,' Maria said. 'Where I grew up we all knew our neighbours.'

'So did we. I still get a little present from the woman next door at Christmas.'

'Now, you see? That's what I'm talking about. That's nice, isn't it?'

'We talked about that, actually,' I said. 'Wished for it even when we moved here. When we first bought the place, like, and were settled. We were envisioning kids. And other kids for them to play with. We thought about having a party.'

'And did you?'

'No. And then we got a bit upset that we got no invites either.'

'Were you expecting fruit baskets?'

'Honestly?' I said. 'I think we were. Something like that. Just a little – what? Something would have been nice.'

'Recognition.' Maria nodded. 'I get that.'

'So, who are you, then?'

'I'm Maria.'

'And Turlough?'

'He's Turlough.'

'Right.'

Maria squirmed. 'I'm a dietician. Turlough's an engineer. I was born in Dublin but grew up in Madrid. Dad taught English. Mammy was a housewife. I came back here for college. That's where I met Turlough. Will that do?'

'Sure.'

'That's better?'

'That's good.'

'That's how people talk to one another, isn't it?'

'As far as I remember.'

Maria smiled. 'And you?'

'I'm Kevin, she's Sarah. Unmarried, no kids.'

'Oh, us too, I forgot that.'

'She's an HR officer, the money of the operation.' I laughed. Maria studied me. 'And she's based in London at the moment.'

'Working?'

'Working.'

'For good?'

'For now.'

'Right.'

'Just for now.'

'Sorry.'

'But we'll work it out.'

'Sure.'

I sipped my tea.

'So,' Maria said after a while. 'What do *you* do for a living? If she's the money, you're the – what?'

'I'm a music journalist.'

'Really?'

'Freelance.'

'So, you're the passion, then?'

'You could say that.'

Maria chewed her lip. She folded her legs beneath her and leaned towards me across the arm of the couch. 'Who do you get to meet? Impress me, now. Is it ever anyone cool?'

'From time to time.'

'Who's the most famous person you ever met?'

I thought for a moment. 'Roy Keane.'

'Is he a musician as well?'

'I was in a queue behind him in an airport.'

Maria grinned. 'So, do you work for a newspaper or a magazine?'

'Internet.'

'Is that what you wanted to be when you were a kid?'

'There was no Internet when I was a kid.'

'I bet you wanted to be in a band.'

'To be honest, no, not really.'

'What, then?'

'I wanted to be an explorer.'

Maria giggled.

'Thanks very much.'

'I'm sorry. That's perfectly reasonable. So, where would you have explored?'

'I never really thought that far ahead.'

'And where would you have lived?'

'I've always liked Dublin.'

Together we looked out the window: grey, heavy sky. When our eyes met I noticed in Maria's a fear with which I was familiar.

'Christ,' she said. 'I can't do this. Just sit here? Come on. We'll have to go look.'

'But what if she comes back by herself?'

'Do you think that's likely?'

I shrugged. 'If she can turn a handle . . .'

'Well.' Maria stood. 'I have to do something.'

I heaved myself from the chair and followed Maria to the hall. She took out her key and swore as she watched it swivel in the lock. She rolled her eyes at me, I shrugged, and together we took the stairs, Maria's hand brushing the banister behind her.

Outside the afternoon was cold, already turning to evening.

'Well, Magellan, which way?' Maria said.

I squinted into the wind, wondering about the dog's motivation. 'This way,' I said, and led us along the alley between our building and the next one. It felt good to be out, breathing fresh air; my steps grew quickly in confidence. But soon I realized that there were parts of the development with which I was unfamiliar: clean canyons sided with unknowable buildings; a mini-plaza built around a waterless fountain; gleaming access roads that ended abruptly at the borders of grass-choked wastelands. At the furthermost edge of the development I stepped into empty space and looked out over churned earth, abandoned digging machinery, stacks of concrete sewer pipes and new snarls of brambles and brush. Maria called the dog's name, and I did too, but the only sound that returned was the trundle of motorway traffic.

I took a step forward into the muck but Maria's hand on my elbow restrained me. 'No,' she said. 'Let's not.'

We trudged back to the front door of the building and sat on the lips of two enormous planters empty of plants. Together we looked across the street through a gap in the hoarding at the stretch of waste ground I had seen from Turlough and Maria's window, which now had been deserted by most of the kids. The few who remained sat on thick-treaded tyres and threw stones at the windows of earth movers.

'Whose kids are they?' I said.

'I don't know.' Maria shrugged. She ran her hand through her hair and gave me a white smile.

I watched the arc of a well-launched stone, heard the shatter of glass and the trill of thin voices swallowed in space. I closed my eyes for a moment and tried to think of Sarah but instead I found myself picturing the dog. First it was a Jack Russell, then a sad-faced boxer, now a golden retriever jumping for a lofted tennis ball, now a greyhound running through tulips.

When I opened my eyes again I saw, at the end of the street, the gloom begin to coalesce into the shape of a figure who could only have been Turlough. The dog was at his heel. I pointed. Maria shouted. The dog broke into a gallop. Earlier, hunting, I had admired the languor of Maria's gait, but now, as she started to run, I saw an awkwardness: she lifted her knees too high, planted her feet too heavily. A few feet from the dog, she dropped to one knee. The dog leaped into her arms. She snuggled it, whispered something in its ear and rose to kiss Turlough. They stood for a moment, his hand in her hair and her hands against his chest. Then they started back, coiled together, the dog trotting in obedient step.

'Told you I'd find her,' Turlough grinned.

'You were right,' I said. 'And fair play to you.'

'I'm sorry,' Maria whispered to him.

'Me too.' He kissed her forehead. 'I'll get a locksmith out tonight.'

I looked down at the dog: a muscular red setter with clouds of steam rising from its coat. The blacks of its eyes flashed white and its pink tongue lolled in slaver.

'Good stuff,' I mumbled. 'Listen, I should get going.'

'Nonsense!' Turlough said and slapped my shoulder. 'You'll do nothing of the sort. You'll have a drink with us. I won't hear no. Come on, now. We're celebrating.'

He led the way back upstairs, ushered us inside and opened the patio door. 'Pull up a pew,' he said as Maria folded herself into a deckchair. 'I'll run in now and open us up a bottle.'

'This'll be nice,' Maria said to the dog. 'Won't it?'

I leaned over the balcony and looked down at the stretch of waste ground, now fully deserted; and beyond that at the halogen fog that signified the city, the red blinking eye at the top of the spire; and, in the distance, a hulking blackness spread beneath the arched spine of the Dublin mountains. I thought of Sarah, far away.

The dog nuzzled the backs of my knees.

'She likes you,' Maria said. 'Don't you?'

The dog shuffled its front paws and licked Maria's outstretched fingers. Turlough came back with three glasses and a bottle of wine. He uncorked the bottle and poured us each a glass.

'Your health,' he said.

We clinked glasses and Turlough leaned back in his deck-chair. He crossed his legs and let a sandal dangle.

I sat forward. 'So, Maria was saying you're an engineer?'

'That's right.'

'What do you work on? Buildings? Bridges?'

'Aircraft.'

'Really?'

'No joke.'

'He's very clever,' Maria said.

'At the airport?'

'Where else?'

I finished my first glass quickly. Turlough topped me up.

'And you're a – what?'

'Music journalist,' Maria said.

'Fancy.'

'Freelance,' I said.

'Still. Sounds creative.'

'I'm sure it is,' Maria said.

Turlough frowned. 'Where can I read you?'

'I have a blog. I'll give you the address.'

'Do.'

'I'd like that too,' Maria said.

Turlough nodded slowly. 'I'd be interested.'

'But he wanted to be an explorer.' Maria smiled at me.

Turlough frowned. 'What are you talking about?'

The dog parted its jaws in a wide-open yawn. It shook its head and stretched itself out flat.

'She's had a long day,' Maria said.

'We all have,' Turlough said.

Maria bit her lip.

'So, you live by yourself?' Turlough said.

'No,' I said. 'Well, yes, at the moment.' I explained my situation.

'It's temporary,' Maria said.

'Good,' Turlough said.

'We might have them up soon? Next time?'

Turlough finished his second glass. 'Sure.'

We killed the bottle. I looked at my watch and made my

excuses. Turlough walked me to the door. As I was passing the kitchen, I saw the parcel sitting on the island, and thought for a moment, until I thought better, to ask him to open it in front of me. Turlough opened the door and I stepped out into the corridor. He spread himself in the doorway, his arm locked solid against the frame. Maria leaned over it to shake my hand. Turlough held firm.

'Don't be a stranger,' he said.

'I won't.'

Maria leaned and nodded. The door closed. I stood for a minute and tried to listen through it but they didn't seem to be speaking.

Back downstairs, buoyed a little from the drink and a little desperate for ceremony, I decided to forgo my usual sans-Sarah meal of noodles or pasta and instead went foraging in the freezer. I found a vegetarian chilli I remembered Sarah having made on one of her first weekends back. I defrosted it in the microwave and, as it heated on the stove, I set the table with a placemat and a plate and arranged cutlery with care. The chilli tasted muddy, freezer-burned and old, but I took massive consolation in its moments of clean spice. When I was done, happy and full, I turned on the computer and searched my music library for a sad, hopeful song that Sarah and I had once spent a long weekend listening to. I played it as loud as I could, and as it played I washed the dishes, moving between sink and cupboard with a tea towel swinging in my hand.

I set my alarm for the next morning an hour earlier than usual, and when I woke I used that time to drink a cup of coffee on the balcony. Then I took a long shower, combed my hair, moisturized the patches of eczema that had begun on my elbows and which I had angered in my sleep. I cut the nails of my fingers and toes and shaved off the patchy beard I had neglected. Afterwards I looked at myself in the bathroom mirror, saw the spread around my waist, and made a resolution to exercise. I threw my sweatshirt and tracksuit bottoms into the wash and dressed in fresh clothes. I emptied the laundry basket into the washing machine and, as the drum whirred, I dismantled the apartment. I repositioned the floor lamps and moved the bookshelves, rearranged the books in ascending order of height. I dusted the TV screen and Windolened the balcony windows. Then I worked all day, with a joy I could only dimly recall. I started an essay I had been thinking about for a long while and finished it over the next few days, during which time I resumed my skype appointments with Sarah – who was snowed under with work in Stockholm, who was sorry she had missed my flowers, who couldn't wait to come home.

I started jogging nightly through the grounds, and by Thursday I noticed an improvement in my breathing. That night, at the edge of the development where Maria had restrained me, I saw her and Turlough and the dog. Turlough was hitting a tennis ball with a hurley for the dog to give chase. His shoulders were powerful, his movements fluid. Maria stood off to one side hugging her elbows and looking out towards the motorway. I waved as I wheezed past but she didn't see me. I ran on.

On Friday morning I sent my essay to the colour section of a weekend newspaper, and that evening I decided to surprise Sarah at the airport. I dressed in the shirt and jacket she always picked for me whenever I asked her advice. I called a taxi and waited for it downstairs. The air was warm and murky with twilight. I sat on the lip of one of the planters and smoked my first cigarette in a week. Behind me the door opened. I turned to see Maria.

'Hi, neighbour.' I grinned.

'Oh, hi.'

She was wearing a thin T-shirt and no make-up. I patted the planter beside me but she didn't move.

'I'm just waiting for a taxi, going to meet Sarah. She's coming in tonight.'

'Good for you.'

'I saw you yesterday playing with the dog.'

'Okay.'

'No more jailbreaks, I presume?'

'No.'

'Come here to me, though, I was meaning to ask you, what was in the parcel?'

Maria shrugged. 'Just some stuff for Turlough. It's not important.'

Her eyes met mine. They were wet and shining. She was, I could tell, in the midst of some new search. I felt compelled to ask about it, to offer her something. I stood, but just then the lights of my taxi appeared at the end of the street. I took a step back from Maria and waved for the driver. The car hitched over a speed bump and eased its way towards us.

'This is me,' I said.

'Okay,' Maria nodded.

'Maybe we'll see you two over the weekend?'

'I'll have to check with Turlough.'

The taxi pulled to a halt beside us. I opened the door and got in.

'Airport,' I said.

'Right you are,' the driver said. He spun us round and pointed the car towards Sarah. I was careful not to look back.

Stag

Goofy on Valium for a lumbar sprain, I hobbled the streets of Midtown. It was early evening, late spring, and the pavements were thronged with open-collared crowds muscling from office to subway. Behind me lay a day's frustration examining bulge-bracket risk assessments; ahead of me a night of TV, back pain, analgesics. On the Lower East Side, Jeanine was bacheloretting with three of her Gamma Phi sisters, all of whom had blown off work to treat her to a spa day. In a week's time, my own half of the wedding party would consist of the sisters' husbands, since the last of my real friends were back home in Ireland and each was too skint to cover air fare or too slammed with work or whatever else.

They were decent guys, the husbands – prep-school types to a man, who wore loafers with no socks, went out to brunch on weekends and spoke in booming, good-timey voices that got boomier and good-timier the more they drank – but they weren't my friends. Neither were the other analysts with whom I chatted solely about work-related topics across cubicle walls, or the guys with whom I played silent, elbowy pick-up basketball on Thursday evenings. I'd told Jeanine that it would be too weird to ask any of them to stand at an altar with me, told her too – when she'd called from the cab between the seaweed wrap and pre-dinner margaritas – that I'd be fine and that I didn't mind not having a stag night. But now I felt homesick and thirsty.

During my first few months in the city, I'd often fled with a book and a flask from the lonely jostle of the streets to the tranquil water and open air of the Bethesda Terrace. I'd stopped needing to do that since meeting Jeanine, yet now – bookless, flaskless – I set a course for the park in hope of finding an hour's escape. I waited to cross Fifty-ninth in the shadow of a grand hotel in whose bridal suite, at my father-in-law's expense, I would soon spend my wedding night. Traffic pulled at my sleeves and dung-stink crowded my nostrils. On the far side of the street, I saw a horse tethered to a hansom cab and, beside it, a figure in the shape of Stephen Quinn. Whenever I was lonely, the faces of New York crowds had a way of throwing up people from home – a half-glimpsed ridge of nose or freckle of cheek that to my mind could belong only to someone who'd been better than me at football or sat beside me in Art. Most of the time, probably, it was a mirage. But this time it really was him.

When we were kids, Stephen and I had been close in a way that I think might be exclusive to friendships between only children of divorce. His mother cooked dinner for me twice weekly, and mine for him, and we hated each other's fathers almost as much as we hated our own. We ran away together, shoplifted together, defended each other in schoolyard battles – and then, the summer we finished school, I spent a night with his girlfriend for reasons I could never fully grasp, and ended up starting college with a partially detached retina and two fractured bones in my right hand. The bones had healed by Halloween, and I suppose Stephen's bruises had too, but he wouldn't take my calls, and by Christmas I stopped calling. It had been almost a decade since we'd spoken, but I knew from Facebook friends of Facebook friends that he and Ciara were still together, and that recently they'd been in the city visiting her sister who was over on a J-1. With Jeanine in the bathroom one evening, I'd stalked my way to Ciara's photo albums and scrolled through them, both glad and disappointed that we hadn't run into each other. I knew now that the sister was back home in Dublin. I hadn't known that Stephen and Ciara had stayed on.

The light changed. I waited. Pedestrians surged past and Stephen approached without seeing me. Was it Valium or loneliness that made me shout his name? His eyes were neutral as they met mine. Then his lips divided in a smile, and we stood for a moment to look each other over. He wore a red hoody, baggy jeans and tightly laced desert boots, all of which appeared to have been picked for nights lounging in beer gardens but had seen too much work and wear. I noticed that he was balding and had grown harder through the shoulders. I noticed him notice my greying temples and swelling middle.

'Well,' he said.

We dispensed quickly with how-have-you-beens and what-are-you-up-to-nows, volunteering little and pretending to know less about each other than we did. We asked about each other's mothers and I asked him how he liked New York. And then, pleasantries over – we were Irish, what else was there? – he said:

'Pint?'

Three avenues to the east, I knew all too well, there was a string of places with walls decked in county colours and juke-boxes stocked with the Fureys and the Clancy Brothers. And a short F train ride to the south there was a dark hole in the wall with the best Guinness in the city on tap. I could smell the resin of the tables, taste the tang of hops in the air, see the glint of light on the optics.

'No,' I said. 'I'm off the stuff.'

'For how long?'

'For good.'

'Jesus.' Stephen sounded scandalized. 'That's a bit drastic, no? How'd you decide that?'

'It was decided for me.'

He grinned. 'Ball-breaker, is she?'

'Who?'

'Your missus.' He shrugged off my look of surprise. 'You're

getting married, yeah? You know the way it is. My Mam met your Mam's neighbour.'

I thought of loose talk in supermarket aisles, coffee-shop eavesdropping on Sunday afternoons. I missed my mother.

'No,' I said – what was the point of lying? 'It was the doctor.'

'Doctor?' Stephen frowned. 'You're not going to tell me you were, what, an alcoholic?'

'They tell us we always are.'

'Jesus.' He held a hand to his mouth to conceal either shock or delight. 'Of all people –'

A toothy kid in a top hat with tassels interrupted Stephen's victory lap to thrust a laminated price list between us.

'Carriage ride?' he said. 'Around the park. Very romantic.'

'Go 'way, you,' Stephen said. 'We're not queers, we're –'

'Old friends.' I waved the kid away. 'I was about to go for a walk in the park, actually,' I told Stephen, eager for any company at all and curious as to what his company might mean. 'Interested?'

He looked beyond me, deep into Fifth Avenue. I followed his gaze and saw a mob of shoppers and a tangle of traffic squeezed between glass buildings and shrouded in silver steam.

'Sure,' he stroked his dark stubble. 'Herself is working around the corner but I'm not picking her up for a while yet.'

We beat a cab off the line and, passing through the cloud of doughy sweetness wafting from a churro stand, made for the entrance to the park. I tried to see in Stephen some of my old excitement about the city, but he walked with the same languid economy as ever; even with my limp it was no struggle to match his pace. Growing up, I'd understood his listless stride as expressing comfort in his surroundings, but now it made him seem stubborn and incurious. As we walked he told me his story: laid off from the garage where he'd worked since school; tourist visas they'd already overstayed; a waitress job for her, a construction gig for him; a month-to-month in Elmhurst. I told him about Jeanine, my lack of stag.

'You poor bastard,' he said, a little too happily. 'But what would you have done anyway, what with your . . . you know?'

'I don't know,' I said. 'I didn't get that far. Pizza?'

'Board games? Orange juice? Sounds like the birthday parties we had when we were nine years old.'

I stumbled on a root and checked my fall with an arm around Stephen's waist. Through his clothes, he was warm and solid.

'What's up with you?' he said.

I told him about the weights I'd been lifting in the run-up to the wedding and the muscle twinge that had laid me up in bed for the past three days.

'Jesus. You're falling apart, lad.'

'Says you, bald as a coot?'

'I'm not bald, it's a solar panel for a . . . what's the joke?'

'A sex machine.'

'So, come here to me, did you at least get any good meds out of it?'

I took the pill bottle from my inside pocket and passed it to him. He squinted at the label, unscrewed the cap and shook a pill into the palm of his hand. He brought the hand to his lips and passed the bottle back. I pocketed it again.

'Are you not having one as well?'

'I'm pacing myself.'

We walked in silence along the mossy bank of a duck pond, below street level and hemmed in by trees. Water moved in slow ripples to the bank. Old men sitting on benches tore up loaves of bread.

'So, how's herself?' I said, to get it out of the way.

'She's grand.' Stephen reached out a hand and watched himself turn it over in the breeze.

We stopped at the crest of the bridge to lean against the wall. Its stone was scored and eaten, its grooves crusted with seed pods. In the water, the buildings of Central Park South reached down towards a failing sun. In the distance, rocks like the backs of whales jutted from the park's green surface, above them the vivid leaves and the grey filigree of branches. I thought I could smell on Stephen the compound of soap and old apples that would always be his mother's house.

'So, let me ask you,' he said, 'why really did you . . . you know?'

Often, in the years since – at the library in Belfield, my cubicle in Citywest or my office in East Midtown – I'd thought of the evening I'd run into Ciara at the pub while Stephen was at work, of our drinking and dreaming aloud about our futures before staggering down towards the beach together. I'd wondered what either of us might have been hoping for. I'd wondered why she'd felt she had to tell him and how he could forgive her but not me. And I'd wondered too where Stephen might be, and what it would be like if we saw each other again. Of course, I'd known that I'd need to have an answer for him. Why didn't I?

'I'm sorry,' I said. 'Honestly, Stephen, I am.'

'Yeah.'

'No really, that's something we're supposed . . . It's something I've wanted to say.'

'Lord,' he spoke through his nose in a rising cadence I remembered from mimicking priests, 'grant me the serenity to accept the things I cannot change and – shit, what's the rest of it? The wisdom?'

'Courage.'

'The courage to – shit. What?'

'Change the –'

'Forget it.'

At our feet, in the breeze, candy wrappers dragged their knuckles against the stone and fingered our ankles. Stephen's lips parted to shape a word but he didn't speak. He flicked a pebble from the wall, and we moved off over the bridge. We crossed a running path and cut through a copse of apple blossoms. On a baseball diamond, two Little League teams were playing. The kids wore bright uniforms, orange versus blue. Without discussing it, Stephen and I sat on a rock that gave us a decent view. I thought of truant afternoons by the cliffs, bottles of strong cider in our schoolbags. The orange team's pitcher stamped the dirt and squinted at the catcher's signals. The wind-up was brief, the pitch itself a blur. The ball slammed into the catcher's mitt as the batter swung at air. The pitcher's mother, a sinewy woman not much older than us, nodded slowly and clapped just once, while other parents, clustered on the bleachers, twisted the corners of their mouths.

'There's always one like that, isn't there?' Stephen said.

'Like what?'

'Like it's a law of the universe or something. Put any group of kids together and one'll always stand out head and shoulders above the rest. Wouldn't you think he'd leave off a bit?'

'I was always shite at sports.'

'Remember your run?'

'It's still my run.'

'All elbows and high knees. What'd we call you?'

'The chicken.'

'The chicken, that's right.'

Stephen flapped his elbows and squawked, and a few of the parents shot us stony glances until I punched him in the arm to stop. The teams changed over. The blue team's pitcher was a beanpole whose jersey bunched around his belt. Soon balls were plinking off bats.

'Come on,' Stephen said, 'or I'll be in trouble.'

He helped me to my feet and we walked to Columbus Circle. A smear of yellow cabs wound around the fountain. High above us, atop his pillar, the stone Genoan stretched a foot into space.

'Well,' Stephen said, 'this was unexpected.'

'It was good,' I said. 'And here, take my number. Give me a shout if you need . . . if you ever want to.'

He punched into his phone the numbers I recited. I watched him hit 'Save' and type the letters of my surname. I took out my phone and waited for him to speak numbers of his own. He looked at it in my hand.

'Sure, I'll see you again,' he said, and I realized that what I'd hoped for was impossible. He thumped me in the biceps and I watched him lope away, thick shoulders rolling as he sought space in the crowd that swallowed him.

A metal globe tilted from a marble plinth beside the subway entrance. Its continents shone, encircled by rings that traced the orbits of things I couldn't see. I rode the 1 to Ninety-sixth where I ground my teeth as I climbed the steps and the grip of Valium weakened. The wind howled across Broadway edged with the dankness of the river. I stopped at a deli on the corner to buy aspirin, bagels for the morning and, at the register, two new bridal magazines to add to Jeanine's collection. As I waited for my change, I tried not to listen to the fridges' hum. Instead I wondered about Stephen and Ciara, and where they might have gone to once he picked her up.

At the door of our building, I nodded hello to Armand from across the hall and retreated from the scent of whiskey rising from his breath. Inside the apartment, I plugged my iPod into the stereo – a habit from when I'd lived alone and grown to fear what I might do with silence. I refilled Jeanine's two-gallon water filter from the tap and, as I manoeuvred it on to the shelf, a shock of pain stole my breath. I closed the fridge door and leaned against it gasping, uncapped the aspirin bottle and swallowed three of them dry. Then I limped to the armchair and lowered myself slowly. I rested my phone on the arm and watched its screen not lighting.

Some hours later I woke to the sound of Jeanine clunking in the hallway. I gripped the arms of the chair and tried to stand but couldn't. She lurched into the room with her hair slung over her eyes, one knee-high boot flapping in her hand and the other still clinging to her calf.

'I'm trapped.' She heaved the booted foot into my lap and braced herself against the bookcase. 'Off. Help.'

I followed the line of her leg to a hard stomach bared just a sliver where her white shirt lifted. The flesh there was pale and taut, both powerful and fine. I swallowed the pain of raising my arms and fumbled with the boot's tiny buckles.

'You'll never guess who I met,' I said.

Jeanine kicked the boot into the base of the sofa and veered towards the stereo. She squinted at the screen of my iPod and spun the wheel to rack up the volume.

'Neighbours,' I warned, picturing the pleated face of the Russian woman in the adjoining unit.

'To hell with the neighbours! Dance with me.'

Her fingers trailed in the air above her head and touched a current she let flow through her limbs. Her hair kicked about her face, her eyes closed, her lips parted. Who had watched her while I waited?

'I can't,' I said.

'What is it?' She yanked the iPod from its cable and dropped to a knee at my side. Her eyes were wet, the pupils yawning. 'What do you need? The doctor? I'll get the doctor.'

'I'm fine. I just need to rest.'

'Okay,' Jeanine swallowed. 'I'll just go puke real quick.'

Through the slats of blinds we'd hung together, I watched the darkened buildings of Ninety-ninth Street. The brickwork was chipped and traffic-blackened, and something white shone from a corner window. I tried to remember the feel of double vision, of a floor tile against my cheek. Jeanine emerged from the bathroom, throat pale, lip bitten. An orange trickle rimmed the collar of her shirt.

'You'll never guess who I met,' I said.

'You know,' Jeanine drifted into the centre of the room, 'it's not really fair that I had such fun at my bachelorette and you never got to have a bachelor . . . No – what do you call it? – a *stag* party.'

Her hips began to sway against remembered music. She dug

her thumbs inside the waistband of her jeans and tugged them over the points of her hips.

'Jeanine,' I said.

'Would you have wanted something like this?'

She backed into me giggling and aimed a kiss across her shoulder. I rested my hands on her thighs and read the Braille of gooseflesh.

'You're freezing cold.' I pulled the blanket from the chair back and held it over her chest.

'I just wanted to dance for you,' she said but her voice was distant, her body still, her eyes already closed.

Until dawn I sat holding on to her as she mumbled to herself and frowned. Her face was red from drink, smudged with make-up, free of worry. A week later we were married. Jeanine's friends wore green and their husbands wore the ties I'd bought for them. We looked good together. Jeanine looked happy. The photographer wanted to take pictures of us in the park but it rained all day.

Two Fires

Thursday evening, five o'clock, Chloe and Julian belly up to the bar of the Terminal 3 Chili's at O'Hare. Palo Alto is four hours behind them; after the layover, it will be two more hours to Boston. Julian orders wings and a beer, Chloe a neat vodka.

They have arrived just in time for happy hour, and the place is filling steadily. The bar stools, and the plastic tables divided from the terminal concourse by a low green fence, are occupied by professional travellers – men and women who pair compact flight cases with soft leather shoes, who curate Delta accounts with miles you could ride to the moon. Some fine-tune presentations on laptops. Others read books with titles like *Your Greatest Asset Is . . . You!* The women mask heavy eyes with subtle make-up. The men tug at ties, slap backs and yell at each other.

'I think,' Chloe says as Julian's food arrives, 'I've figured out what my problem is.'

'Oh yeah? After all this time?'

Between Julian's fingers, the wings feel gnarled and oily. Their skin is a hi-vis shade of orange. He gulps his beer against their spice and tries with a flailing arm to catch the attention of the bartender, a swollen old walrus with two dozen enamel buttons affixed to his red suspenders, but the walrus just stares right through him and nods at Chloe as she indicates the suds in Julian's glass with a purple-nailed finger.

'Am I invisible, here?'

Chloe shrugs. She is five-foot-three in heels, but every meeting is dominated at all times by her presence. Tomorrow morning, the two of them will pitch for a social media campaign worth somewhere in the high six figures, and she will take the lead.

'I think,' she says, pulling a celery stem from Julian's basket and beginning to suck it, 'that fundamentally, I find men repulsive.'

The walrus sets a fresh beer in front of Julian and slopes away. Julian drinks thirstily between mouthfuls of deep-fried flesh.

'I mean, I like the idea of men, or of *a* man. The Platonic concept of man is something I can get right behind.'

'Right, right.' Julian adds to the dolmen of chicken ulnas teetering on his side plate.

'But these earthly men with whom I have to deal? These shadows on the walls of the cave? They just leave me cold, I'm afraid. I find them . . . somewhat lacking.'

Julian leans back in his stool and wipes from his forehead a smear of grease vaguely scented with cayenne pepper.

'That's a shame,' he says. 'But wait, what about the chef?'

'Drug habit,' Chloe says.

'Coke?'

'Meth.'

'Huh.'

'You sound so shocked.'

'I'm not,' Julian says. 'Were you?'

'Not really,' Chloe smiles. When she sips her drink, she reaches first for the straw with her tongue. Her vodka, slow and viscid, oils the side of her glass. 'But what about you? You're still out there, right? Sometimes? Still giving it the old college try?'

'Still am, yes. Despite past experience.'

'You, my friend,' Chloe aims the celery stem at Julian and sights along its length, 'are an optimist.' She chomps down with a snap and speaks through a full mouth. 'That's what I've always liked about – Oh God!'

Her hand shoots to cover her lips. Julian turns to see what she sees. And there, billowing from the kitchen hatch, is a cloud of purplish smoke. Beyond it Julian can make out many tongues of blue and orange flame.

'It's a bomb!' someone shrills, with sad inevitability. And with that, screams are torn from anguished throats, drinks spilled and plates sent crashing as people fumble for bags, slam laptop lids, elbow each other.

'It's all right, it's all right,' the walrus shouts, and Julian is convinced in an instant of raw lung power that this man has spent time in the military.

A busboy in a white smock rushes through the swinging door and discharges a fire extinguisher. Light smoke replaces the dark and something somewhere sizzles.

'It's just a little grease fire,' Sergeant Walrus reassures. 'Everything is under control.'

Collective relief is sighed, disappointed and guilty. Julian looks towards his trembling hand and realizes that it, without his conscious agency, has settled on the smooth skin and angular bone of Chloe's knee. He snaps it back.

'Sorry, I –'

But he stops himself, for now he is looking into her eyes and what he sees there is something he never would have expected.

'The next round's on the house,' the walrus shouts.

Collective cheers. Julian flails an arm. Chloe gestures with a finger.

Already this year, the firm has doubled revenue, and last month *Forbes* did a feature on Chloe as part of its '30 Under 30' series. Still, she and Julian are just eighteen months removed from business school and have agreed to reinvest the majority of whatever they bank into growing the business. The hotel in Back Bay is a little pricier than either of them would have liked, but the pitch meeting is early and they don't want a repeat of the Cleveland RTA nightmare.

'Checking in together tonight?' the desk clerk says. She is young and bored and attractively plain, the set of her lips poised on the cusp of gossip.

'Yes,' Julian says. 'But separate rooms.'

'Of course, sir.'

The clerk clickety-clacks her keyboard in search of their reservation, and Julian knows, as he has done at numerous other reception desks in numerous other cities, exactly what she is thinking. There is something, he supposes, about the way he and Chloe stand together, an enhanced awareness of each other's space honed by three years of studying and working and travelling together.

The clerk, with a hollow-cheeked smile, hands over keys for adjoining rooms on the sixth floor.

'Come on, *dah*-ling,' says Chloe, her voice hoarse from travel, and leads Julian to the elevator where Glenn Miller bleats from the speakers. She hums along as she reads emails on her phone. 'You hungry?' she says, without looking up. 'I'm peckish.'

'I told you,' Julian tells her, 'to eat something real in Chicago.'

'But everything there was icky-gross.'

'You think you'll find non-gross food anywhere at this hour? What time is it?'

'Eleven seventeen,' Chloe says, 'but I'm still on West Coast time.'

The elevator doors open on a taupe hallway hung with pictures of smoky shipyards. Chloe checks her room number and sets off wheeling her case.

'If I go to the bar,' Julian says, 'I'll drink.'

'So, drink.'

'But I want to be clear in the morning.'

'So, don't drink.'

'It's just that easy for you, isn't it?'

'Well, I'll order room service, then,' Chloe says, dipping her key card and jiggling the handle. 'Come drink. Or don't drink. Or eat. Or don't eat.'

In his room, Julian unpacks his suit and hangs it to de-crease. He lays out an undershirt and underwear and socks. Through the wall, he listens to Chloe murmuring, most likely to her mother in Portland, who hasn't been well, and who Chloe has called every night without fail since Julian has known her. He changes into sweatpants and his red Stanford sweatshirt and lies on the bed to watch CNN. The news cycle is dominated by a hurricane that has hit the Florida Keys. Julian watches footage of palm trees bending, rowboats in the street.

When he hears another voice in Chloe's room, he kills the TV and gets up to knock on the adjoining door.

'Go Cardinal!' Chloe laughs, pointing to his sweatshirt.

The room-service guy is old and thin and smiling. He bows when Julian tips him and walks backwards from the room. On Chloe's bed lies a tray containing a chopped salad, a brioche roll and two bottles of Diet Coke.

'Will we rehearse this one last time?' she says.

'Why?' They have gone over the pitch together so many times in the past few days that anyone, Julian thinks, would know it backwards by now. 'Something isn't bothering you, is it?' he says. 'The unflappable, the indefatigable . . .' But he trails off because he sees that Chloe's lips are taut.

'It's my mom,' she says. 'Her insurance is just, like . . . Something about a fucking pre-existing condition . . . I just – I really need this to go well right now.'

She is within arm's reach; he could hug her, he thinks, or lay a hand between her shoulder blades.

'Well, then,' he says. 'Let's fire it up.'

Chloe nods once, twice, then touches each cheek lightly with her fingertips. She tugs her T-shirt over her hips and opens her laptop on the desk.

'Good morning,' she says, and at once the stiffness of worry leaves her body; her back is straight, her arms are loose, her chin is high.

She hits her PowerPoint marks cleanly each time, cycling through slides without ever glancing at the screen; spouts fluently the figures that Julian has projected; speaks urgently, persuasively; asks rhetorical questions. Julian knows that even if he weren't the only other person in the room, she still could make him feel as though he were.

'And that's the game,' he tells her, exactly twenty-three minutes later. He holds a hand high in the air for her to five it. Chloe stretches to throw a jab into his open palm and shadow-boxes on the spot.

Julian twists the cap from a Diet Coke and hands it to her. Chloe makes a fist around the bottle, and for a moment they both watch the cables of her white arm bulge and release, bulge and release.

'Hey, Chlo?' he says.

'Yeah?'

'Are you going to eat your roll?'

The sky is low over Dartmouth Street. A salt wind rolls in off the Charles. Chloe's hair sails behind her, and her jacket, caught on her shoulder-bag strap, rides up to reveal the brass-toothed zipper of her skirt. On Boylston Street, she and Julian join the progress of commuters rising from the Copley T stop and hurrying headlong through the wind towards their offices.

Outside the public library, a raw-boned man in military fatigues dances a one-legged jig and shakes a can. The sky is clear but cold and the last of the winter's snow lingers on the library steps in diminished heaps. Chloe and Julian enter the Prudential Center, a great biodome of chain-store shopping and food-court dining. At the Tower lobby, they give their names to a desk clerk who furnishes them with visitors' passes and leads them to the elevators.

'Ready?' Julian says as the floors tick up.

'As I'll ever be,' Chloe says.

'Here,' he reaches for her jacket, 'you're snagged.'

'I've got it,' she says and steps away from his hand.

The offices of Bobst and Law are spread across three floors, the conference room located at a corner of the seventeenth. Chloe connects her laptop to a projector at the head of the table while Julian takes a seat and pours himself a glass of water.

The CMO, Tom Bobst, convenes the meeting. The nephew of the founder, he looks to Julian as though he skis yearly, golfs weekly, and climbs mountains for fun. He is trim and tall, with a big toothy face. His blue jacket is nipped at the waist and short in the arm to show monogrammed cuffs. His watch, undoubtedly, cost more than Julian's last two cars. Flanking him are a short bald man from Compliance, with bulging eyes and a collar at least half an inch too tight, and a woman from Fiscal whose glasses have thick frames and whose eyes Julian can't see because they are locked on her phone.

'Good morning,' Chloe says.

The conference room has two glass walls that give on to an open bullpen crammed with cubicle-jockeys, and two floor-to-ceiling windows overlooking the Boston skyline. As Chloe speaks, Julian watches for the moments when the Bobst people

take notes and scribbles answers on a legal pad for the questions they will ask. Beyond Chloe he can see the clay roof of
Trinity Church in Copley Square, the collegey-graveyardy
stillness of the Common and the golden dome of the State-
house winking from the hillside. And for a moment, he pictures
himself living here, in a tight Beacon Hill brownstone or a big
old Cambridge Queen Anne; sees himself riding the T each
morning to a salaried job that demands fewer than eighty hours
per week, spending weekends in some mall or other. He has
never before wanted regularity; the 'intense, think-tank atmos-
phere' of the Palo Alto office is not only, as *Forbes* wrote, a key
to Chloe and Julian's way of business, it also has been the key
to his way of life. But this other life enjoyed by the people
assembled here this morning – he sees now how it could offer
a different kind of reward.

'Now,' Chloe says when she has finished, 'I'll turn you over
to my colleague.'

Four sets of eyes ratchet in Julian's direction. His hand
shakes slightly as he distributes supporting materials in cobalt
folders embossed with his and Chloe's company logo, but
when he turns to actionable time frames and real-world deliv-
erables, his voice is steady. He fields questions that fall within
his purview and hands off to Chloe those that fall within hers.
He cracks wise with the compliance guy about the Celtics and
invites them all to a Warriors game next time they find themselves in the Bay Area.

'Well,' Bobst smiles, 'you've certainly given us a lot to think about.'

'It's been our pleasure,' Julian says.

As he is heading out the door, he realizes that Chloe isn't following. She sits on the edge of the conference table, legs crossed at the knee and a foot wagging. Bobst leans above her with a palm stretched flat by her thigh. She presses his wrist and nods her head and opens her throat to laugh.

'Chlo?' Julian says.

The smile on Bobst's face freezes.

'She'll catch you up,' he says.

'I'll wait for you in the lobby.'

'I might –' Chloe says. 'I'll see you at the hotel, okay?'

'I'll walk you out,' the compliance guy says, his hand brisk at Julian's elbow. 'And what about baseball? Can you get good seats for the Giants when the Sox are in town?'

Julian tells him, 'The best.'

He had hoped for the opportunity to wander around the city a bit between meeting and flight, maybe eat a celebratory steak with Chloe in one of the places on Stuart Street, but now, back at the hotel, Julian finds his energy drained, his appetite depleted. He calls down to reception to arrange for late check-out, then changes into his travelling clothes – good jeans, a collared shirt – and packs his suit and shoes. Out the window he can see the Prudential Tower's severity of glass and angle. What the hell could Chloe still be talking about in there?

As someone who reads signs and makes predictions for a living, Julian hates it when he misses things – has he missed something?

He goes to the bathroom, fills the sink and dunks his face. Water runs in ribbons down his nose and cheeks. He towels off, breathing slowly. He brushes his teeth against the bitter taste that has gathered on his tongue, then slumps on to the bed and grinds his teeth and presses a thumb into his eye. He turns on the TV to a hotel station where a man in full colonial dress stands in the lobby of a seafood restaurant. The camera zooms in on a bowl of bubbling chowder. A cartoon lobster with rubber bands around its claws scuttles happily across the screen and winks.

After a while, through the wall, Julian hears the click of Chloe's door.

Then the second fire starts. The alarm begins as a low, two-tone hum out in the hallway, after which Julian hears a series of heavy clunks that he understands to be the fire doors falling shut.

'Christ,' he mutters, thinking drill or false alarm, but pockets his phone and his wallet just in case. He tries to open the adjoining door but it won't budge.

'Hey, Chlo?'

There is no answer. He goes out into the hallway where the alarm is louder – its low notes hoarse, its high notes shrilling – and knocks on Chloe's door.

'Hey, Chlo? Come on, Chlo, I think this might be serious.'

A family from the far end of the hallway hurries towards him. The children, a little girl and a little boy, are in pyjamas; hers – weirdly, Julian thinks – have pictures of football players on them, while his have pictures of ponies. And now all of the phones in all of the rooms are ringing. And now all of the lights fail and it is dark. The emergency lights flick on and everything is blue and nocturnal and submarine. The little girl screams and the little boy whimpers.

'It's okay,' the father says.

'We're just going on a little adventure,' the mother says.

Chloe's door opens. 'Jesus Christ,' she says, the skin of her face blue and in her eyes the same thing Julian saw at the airport.

She starts towards the elevators but Julian reaches for her hand and leads her towards the stairs instead. In the stairwell it is very hot and very loud. The air is dense with smoke. Women in suits and men in bathrobes join them at each landing. Julian's heels are stepped on. Someone breathes in his ear. They make it to the lobby where hotel employees wave their arms and shout directions. Firefighters in heavy coats hustle through the lobby doors. And now everyone is running, pushing over potted ferns and leatherette chairs and ottomans and each other.

Julian's shoulders and knees are jostled and his grip on Chloe's hand strains and, finally, breaks.

He turns to look for her but, as he does, the woman in front of him trips and falls and he slams into her hip and vaults over her shoulder. He lands with an elbow jammed under his ribs; someone's leg falls across his shoulder blades and flattens his lungs. He drags himself to his feet and looks around for Chloe but he can't see her. He tries to push back the way they've come but there are too many people and they are moving too quickly. Their eyes are too wide. They push and they keep pushing.

'No returns,' a firefighter shouts and points to the door. 'You need to get out. Sir, you and everyone need to get out right now.'

The sidewalk is crammed but firefighters are shepherding people behind a tape perimeter the police are scrambling to roll out at a block's distance in both directions. Julian backs towards it, craning his neck up to see gouts of smoke eddying from the hotel's top three floors. There is something sinister, he thinks, about a fire in the daytime; the clarity of dark smoke against blue sky is awful. He can see shards of curtains waving, individual lampshades aflame and, a floor below them, identical curtains and lampshades waiting.

Behind the barrier, he takes out his phone to call Chloe but the network is down or the tower overwhelmed. Police sirens scream and fire engines honk. Overhead, already, a news chopper is whirling, and on the corner, two crews of EMTs have unloaded gurneys from the backs of ambulances parked at hasty angles. The EMTs stack the gurneys with oxygen canisters and heavy medical bags and fistfuls of supplies wrapped in pale blue plastic. One of the bags bursts and rains pipettes to the ground. A roll of gauze falls free and bounces and unspools. Sitting on a kerb, Julian sees now, is Chloe.

As he runs to her, he notices the bright stream of blood dribbling at her temple. She holds a hand to her head and is missing her left shoe. Julian is standing next to her before she recognizes him. She looks up at him and frowns.

'Are you okay?' he says. 'Boy. Two fires in two days.'

'Yes,' she says, but her face is uncomprehending.

'That has to mean something?'

'Are you hungry?' Chloe says.

Julian kneels beside her and folds his arms around her shoulders. He lays his cheek against hers; and he holds on, even as she tries to pull away, tight.

A Vigil

Whenever things got too much for me, during those bad years when we lived on Harrington Street, I used to leave the flat and go out walking for as long as it took to get my head together. Usually a quick stomp around the block would do the trick, but sometimes I would be gone for hours, marching in aimless fury or boarding buses with a vague desire to spread my anger thin over distance.

No matter where my rambling took me, though, I'd always finish up in the same place. Before going home I'd buy a pack of cigarettes and sit on a bench by the Grand Canal to smoke a few, end to end. I had a favourite spot: just beyond Baggot Street Bridge, where the towpath sinks below the level of the road and is separated from the pavement by a tall black fence. There I could expect to find the silent company of a drunk embracing a bottle of strong cider, or on weekends that of an unimaginative father watching a son or daughter pelting the swans with bits of bread. I liked it down there. It was a place where you could be by yourself without having to suffer the horror of being alone.

Laura, my wife, was an actor, and she was beautiful. If you had seen us together on the street you would have wondered what she saw in me. The answer was that we shared a secret – call it faith or fantasy. What had bonded us in college was a resolution to deny the signs that neither of us was meant for greatness, and it was this commitment that had tightened us together throughout the ruin of our twenties. What did we fight about? The usual, I suppose. Sex, money, selfishness. *Why* we fought is a far more interesting subject, and a problem that I have never quite been able to solve. It certainly didn't help that we were both only ever partially employed, but I think it went deeper than that. I think it had something to do with needing someone to hate every now and then. It also might have had something to do with needing someone to forgive you. Let's just say that in our own ways we were a source of comfort for each other, through our failures and through our shared loss of youth, and that of lesser things are lasting marriages made.

During the week I turned thirty, I studied the Facebook accounts of old friends who had become actuaries or engineers. That weekend Laura arranged for us to spend a few days in her uncle's caravan in Wexford. We drank spiced rum, played songs on my guitar and ate ice cream topped with hundreds and thousands by the beach. We had a decent time. But on the train home on Sunday afternoon we both were dangerously hung-over. We got to sniping and, as soon as we had climbed the stairs to the flat, we fell into a fight. Laura had left her phone behind in the caravan and, as was her wont whenever faced with a problem that lacked an easy solution, she started stomping around the place, slamming doors and working herself into a tantrum.

'But you don't under*stand*,' she said in response to my attempts at soothing her. 'I'm expecting a *call* this week. I'm expecting my *agent*. I'm expecting *work*. Remember work?'

'Sure I remember work,' I said. 'It's the place I go to every day. And where I'll be tomorrow while you're crying over your fucking phone.'

For these were our established starting positions, the pattern we had well rehearsed. Whichever one of us had a job at any given moment would – as well as paying off the credit cards and buying too much shopping from the good supermarket – assume it as his or her right to lord it over the other. Every now and then, I was a productive member of society while she was a spoiled little girl with silver-screen delusions. And occasionally, she was a pillar of financial stability while I was a fantasist who had never quite got over the time his band had opened for – whoever.

Laura moved to the window and began to smoke violently, her chin thrust forward in her customary challenge to the world. She was wearing a pair of my jeans and her skin still smelled of the beach. Stray strands of her hair seemed to glow in the weakening sunlight.

'I'd hardly call what you're doing *work*,' she said. 'Little office boy. That's fucking drudgery.'

I closed my eyes and breathed slowly through my nose. Something in my jaw was clicking back and forth. I struggled for eloquence. I knew where we would be in a few minutes' time but I forged ahead regardless.

'Sweetheart,' I said as my hand sought warmth at the small of her back. 'Look, it's fine. We'll figure it out. Why don't you just call *him*?'

'Oh, right. Yeah, sure. Perfect.' I could tell that Laura was close to tears. 'You really haven't a fucking clue about the world, have you? You really don't know anything about how things work.'

The traffic noise from the street outside had risen to a horrible pitch. It came like a flood through the open window, pulling with it its grime and its threat and forcing me to see my home for what it was. I looked around at the cheap sticks of inexpertly repaired furniture, the battered TV, the maniac watercolours that Laura and I had made together in a shared fit of painterly enthusiasm as – *wham!* – a bus tore past and filled the room with its roar.

In a blind rage I hit the street and walked without direction. The faces of the people walking towards me – strangers on their way to their evening's destinations, where they would be happy, or not – seemed to possess knowledge of how I was living my life. I retreated to a pizza place on Merrion Row and was reassured for a while by the easy comfort of cheese and grease and dough. I ordered beer and moved on to wine and finished with amaretto.

When the waitress came over with my bill she smiled in a way that I thought spoke of pity born from a kindred sadness. She had eyes that looked as though they might never be too far away from crying. I noticed that she was wearing a coat.

'You're finished with your shift,' I said.

Her eyes darted to the door.

'Will you have a drink with me, then? It's my birthday. One drink? I even know a place.'

I could see the rest of the night laid out before us. We would go to the canal together with a bottle and talk until dawn, confess our sins and be reborn in one another's mercy. But of course the waitress wouldn't come with me. What she did was call the manager – a fat, oily little creature with a thick bunch of keys hanging from his belt and a name tag that read 'Eugene' pinned over one of his breasts – who escorted me from the premises and suggested that it might be best if I never returned.

So I bought a bottle of supermarket Cabernet and went alone to the canal. There was no one else on the towpath. It was getting dark but the sky held no hope of stars. I found my usual bench and sat down and opened the bottle. The wine was of the kind that coats your tongue and makes you spit blue for hours. I watched the swans, counting and recounting them, and felt as though I had arrived at a moment of great decision. The feeling had an intensity the like of which I had known only once before. That had been many years earlier, but it was a moment to which my mind often returned while sitting by the canal. Laura and I were still spending our Sunday afternoons in bed back then. I had money, and had just returned from the good supermarket with lunch things I knew she'd like. I found her asleep, the sheets pulled back to reveal her narrow shoulder blades and her head resting on an arm, her face turned towards me. I knew for certain that she was my life and decided right then that I would commit myself to the service of her happiness. Now, as I drank, I tried to picture the way Laura's face had looked that day that made me love her. I focused my mind on trying to pull that image forward from my lost years. But it wouldn't come.

The swans moved off together downstream but one stayed where he was. I watched him closely. An enormous cob, his neck was as long as my arm and above his beak there was a fat black bulge that might have been the source of his power. Soon I began to think that he must be trapped or snagged on something. I walked to the edge of the bank and peered down into the dark water, looking for a snarl of rope or wire or a spear of steel broken from a shopping trolley. There was nothing there, and then there was something. Floating into focus, I began to make out another swollen curl of breast and feather on the bed of the shallow canal. I could see an orange foot, a silt-brown tail. I studied the way the water rocked her neck.

The cob circled slowly, his head tucked tightly to his breast. I decided to make an observance. I sat back down and finished my wine and kept him company until dawn. All night he kept up his slow circling and I was glad that I could be with him. In the morning, as I walked home to end my marriage, I felt as though I might have made a difference in the world. Never since has my life been any better.

Occupations

Before Mallorca, I'd spent six years running the City Lounge on Dawson Street for a Kildareman named PJ Nolan. The heir to a horse-breeding empire, PJ collected pubs and restaurants up and down the country, and sometimes further afield, but he didn't concern himself with our operations so long as we made him money. I was hired to be the head barman but ended up doing everything: ordering stock, rostering staff, paying taxes, booking Christmas parties – plus I pulled pints twenty-six nights out of the month. I spent my days off planning VIP events. The skin around my nails was chapped and smelled of slops. Half my pay went straight to my landlord. I was thirty-three.

I sold my car, took out a loan and bought the lease on Molly Malone's, a cantina situated just off the Paseo del Mar in Palma Nova. For years, the pub had served a pair of package holiday resorts that now were going to be redeveloped into higher-end timeshares. It was a hokey enough place but it had potential, with the promise of strong foot traffic to come and a view – if you leaned over the patio wall and craned your neck – of the glimmering skin of the Med. I ripped out the useless copper piping from above the bar, tore down the vintage Lisdoonvarna posters and Galway street signs, installed onyx tables and leather banquettes and hired a tapas chef. I worked seventeen-hour days, slept in a windowless room upstairs and learned just enough Spanish to shout at tradesmen. I was happy, I think.

But supplier delays and red tape meant that we opened too late to make the most of the high tourist season. And then, when the developer defaulted on payments to the city the following March, the whole district fell into a kind of un-redeveloped limbo. First, the binmen stopped coming and the bags piled up in stinking heaps at the back door. Then, the postman stopped coming and we missed notices from the electricity company and were without power for a long weekend. Finally, my handful of steady off-season customers stopped dragging their pink expatriate flesh from their villas to my stools. I was left with little choice but to shut the doors, sell on the lease for a pittance and return home sorely chastened and deep in debt.

When I called PJ to see about going back to work for him, it turned out that he'd run into problems of his own. He had gambling debts, he said, and problems with the Revenue, but he was still in the game and said he'd be in touch. While waiting for his call, I got drunk on the dole for a few months before I ran into Declan Watts, an old mate of mine from school who was on his way to Australia. He told me that he'd been driving a van for the Department of Justice, ferrying lads around and supervising graffiti removal. 'I'm getting out of here while I can,' he said, 'but if you like, I'll put in a good word for you.'

A week or so later, I got a call offering me an interview. I bought a suit and passed the test for my category D licence. Then it was up at six o'clock Monday to Friday and into the van and off to Mountjoy or the central pickup place on the quays near Tara Street station, where anywhere between two and seven dishevelled-looking lads would be shuffling their feet waiting for me. They'd pile in, I'd call the roll and off we'd go to Fairview or Cabra or wherever the docket said. I had a boot-ful of chemicals I topped up at the depot each week, as well as a collection of buckets and gloves and overalls. We'd pull up to the site, I'd hand out the gear and the lads would get changed and start scrubbing away at spunking dicks or swastikas or mis-spelled paramilitary rubbish. It was nasty work, freezing our holes in the wind and the rain – but it was steady.

The lads were eejits mostly, prone to backchat and a little given to skiving, but I didn't mind them. Generally, they were grateful they'd avoided a custodial sentence. What had they done? Little stuff: too many unpaid parking tickets, shoplifting, public drunkenness. There were also car thieves and small-time drug dealers who would have been locked up if the jails hadn't been so overcrowded. And there was the odd white-collar fellow too, a banker or a lawyer who'd fudged his taxes and got caught out or missed too many upkeep payments to an ex-wife. I dealt with them all the same way: took no messing, listened to no excuses, intervened in no arguments unless I absolutely had to. Of course, it helped that in the back of each of our minds was the sure knowledge that if they took liberties there'd be a report to the parole officer, and that report would almost certainly land them in prison.

During my third or fourth month on the job, the Department rotated me and three other lads out to an unfinished office building on the quays. With me were Tony, who had been an accountant before the recession (and a divorce, a breakdown and a drink-driving charge); Graham, a general delinquent whose uncle, he said, controlled half the heroin in Dublin; and Kevo, a pillhead and serial pisser-in-public – all three of them had been on my crew for a fortnight. The office building had been intended for some tech or consulting outfit. It was little more than a concrete shell, with two glass walls overlooking the Liffey and the bridge, and two blind walls at the back. A few lads had broken in one night and painted it top to bottom. But this wasn't your usual smash of ugly letters. These guys were out to create.

On the pillars on either side of the gaping entrance, they'd painted potted plants stretching their thin branches towards the ceiling. They'd painted architecture, furniture, and they'd painted people too, dozens of them criss-crossing the lobby walls on their way to and from their offices with ID cards on lanyards swinging from their necks. On the rear wall there was a bank of lifts, the doors of one of which were being held open by a tall man for two young women. And beside that there was a high reception desk where three girls answered phones and typed at computers and conversed with visiting conference delegates.

We climbed the stairs, our hands touching those of painted fellow-climbers. On the walls of each floor we found row upon row of desks with computers and in-trays, filing cabinets, photocopiers, printers, water coolers and partition walls cordoning off the offices of managers. Sitting at each of the desks or walking in the aisles between cubicles with cups of coffee in hand or portfolios of papers under arm were people dressed in business suits. They were very thin and very tall. Their faces were blank but you could tell from the way they carried themselves that they were successful and confident and that they worked well as a team, that they were happy doing their work in the time allotted them to do it.

'Suppose all this is familiar to you,' I said to Tony.

He rested one hand on his belly and stroked his loose jaw with the other. 'Not so much, no. Ours was a boutique firm.'

'Yeah,' said Graham, 'and three-dimensional too, I'd imagine?'

'We worked out of a Georgian townhouse in Sandymount.'

'Go 'way.' Graham's dirty hand slapped the shoulder of Tony's polo shirt; Tony winced. 'I robbed one of them once. Tell me now, did yours have double glazing?'

'I think so, yes.'

Graham licked his wispy moustache. 'See, that's what's known as a false economy, there. You put in double glazing to save money on the heating but the old frames just can't take them. Shoulder-nudge and they pop right out.'

The lads struggled into their overalls and Graham and Kevo had a last smoke. In each of their buckets I poured chemicals from a plastic jug with a black X on its side, turning my head against the fumes that rose to my eyes and stung. I took brushes and scouring pads from the van, found a water main and attached the hose. The lads sprayed down the walls and started scrubbing. I took the ladder from the van so they could reach the higher-up parts. Graham climbed and Tony held the ladder steady. Kevo stood off to one side to hose and mop the run-off.

'All set?' I said.

'Leaving us again?' said Tony.

I'd learned quickly that these lads worked well together if I wasn't around and there was no authority to challenge.

'I trust you,' I told them.

'Big mistake,' Graham said and flashed me an evil smile.

I went for a walk down the quays as far as the old Point Depot, looking in along the way at all the new and empty buildings. I had a smoke, passed a pub, thought about going inside but decided against it. Since Mallorca, I was often gripped when passing a pub by an urge to go into the warm dark, order a pint and sit and watch the place in motion: the barman taking stock, pulling pints, conversing; the floor girls bustling about with orders, flirting for tips. I'd study the set-up, note the spirit selection, eye the menu if they had one. I'd trace the grain of the wood and test the give of the upholstery, try to absorb the ambience and figure out what had gone wrong for me.

On the second day I gave in to the urge and spent the morning in an early house. I came back furry-mouthed and light-headed to find Tony and Graham carrying on a shouted conversation from either side of the second floor. Kevo was working away by himself. I gave him some money and told him to run and get the lunches.

'Rolls okay, lads?' I said.

'Grand for me,' Graham said. 'Tony'd prefer sushi, though.'

'Shut up, you,' Tony said with a chuckle.

'In more of a tapas mood, is it?'

I put on a spare pair of overalls and took over from Kevo.

'We were just talking about the Chauvet Cave,' Tony said. 'I saw a documentary about it.'

'And me too,' Graham said. 'No cultural slouch, this one. Did you see it yourself?'

'No,' I said.

'Mad film. 3D. See it whacked if you can. Bonkers.'

'A great piece of cinema,' Tony said with a sage nod. 'Werner Herzog.'

He was a man who liked to think of himself as a connoisseur of the finer things. In two weeks I'd already heard him discourse on Californian fusion cooking, German philosophy and Chinese opera. He loved hearing himself talk. But whenever he got going you sensed trouble, since most topics led him inexorably to the subject of his ex-wife, with whom he used to go to the theatre and the RHA and the restaurants on Merrion Row. As well as the house and the kids, she'd got the season tickets and the memberships.

'Yeah, it's good all right,' Graham said, 'but the paintings were a bit rubbish.'

'What are you talking about?' Tony said, his nose wrinkled as though he'd smelled something rotten. 'They're thousands of years old. They're documentary evidence of man's earliest artistic attempts.'

'Exactly.' Graham was working away. 'So imagine how much better we've all got since then.'

'Art buff, are you, Graham?' I said.

'Sure these –' he gestured to the walls. 'These are better than that.'

'My arse,' Tony said.

'Course they fucking are. 'Cause they're up to date, you know? And they're about things you'd recognize. What would I give a fuck about cows and mammoths and shite for?'

'But can you appreciate,' Tony said, 'the poetry in that? In the very act of describing animals, man proves to himself that he is greater than they, that he is something different, set apart, with a soul and maybe a destiny. It's the fact that they're old that makes them interesting, Graham.'

'It's the fact that these are interesting, Tony, that makes them interesting.'

Kevo came back with our rolls. I took the portable radio from the van and we listened to it as we ate. I liked to save the radio for the afternoons, since the best work always got done in the mornings but only without distractions. In the afternoons, everyone got restless and likely to slow down. Then the radio helped things move quicker; it kept us all focused and honest.

'So, who do you think made them?' Graham said.

'Students,' Tony said. 'Somebody like that.' He was frowning, circling some silent pain.

'Like an anarchist collective?' Graham's eyes were wide and wondering. 'A syndicalist cadre of counter-cultural free-thinkers?'

'Someone like that.'

'Mad.' Graham chewed a hunk of bread and chicken goujons.

'And what does it mean, do you think?' I said.

'It means nothing,' Tony said irritably, his voice rising.

'It has to mean something,' Graham said.

'Why does everything have to mean something?'

When we'd finished eating, I sent the lads back to work and bundled up our rubbish. I took the stairs down to the street, found a bin and stuffed in the wrappers and bags. I was just about to go back inside when I felt a presence, someone watching me. He was standing across the street in the gloom of the bus shelter against the Liffey wall: a tall, thin man dressed all in black. I couldn't see his face.

I'd never noticed before how much graffiti there was in the city. But now I worked for the Department it was inescapable – I saw it everywhere. There was the street-art stuff: a grey wall in an Inchicore estate, say, with a big hole painted in the middle through which you could see a picture-perfect Connemara field. Or the two young, red-eyed cops smoking bongs on a Cow's Lane hoarding. Or the little girl in the polka-dot dress suspended by an umbrella halfway up the wall of a Lidl, either falling or flying, the expression on her face the perfect balance of terror and delight. Then there was the advertising masquerading as art on the hoardings near Richmond Street bridge. There were the pub doors on South William Street with recreated Andy Warhols, and the U2 shrine on Windmill Lane whose appeal I'd never understood. Whenever I got the train to see my mother, I'd look out along the red-brick bridges towards Maynooth and try to decipher the tags, peer into the patches of waste ground near Howth Junction and read the faces of abandoned shipping containers. And on the sides of every community centre, on every alleyway wall, on the fences of every electricity substation, on the glass of every bus stop, I'd see the dregs: the tricolours, the Burn the Rich, the X is a faggot, the Y waz ere.

'It's all just so impotent,' Tony said. This was on Wednesday afternoon.

'You are,' Graham said. 'Will you hold that ladder steady?'

'Who's your favourite?' Kevo said.

We were on the third floor, the lads working away at erasing a desk full of executive toys and framed photos of blank-faced children.

'Favourite what?' Tony said.

'Favourite one of these here pictures.'

'Don't make me laugh. They're rubbish, the lot of them.'

Graham thought for a while. 'That girl over there,' he said and pointed behind him. 'The one with the short skirt and the tight stripy shirt. She's a cracker, a real goer. You can see it in the way she carries herself. I'd bend her over that desk and give her —'

'She's a drawing,' Tony said.

'A drawing who wants it. You can see it.'

'She doesn't even have a face.'

'You have to read between the lines.'

'She's only lines!'

'I liked the lobby,' Kevo said.

'What about the lobby?' I was mopping a pool of water and paint that recently had been two cubicle walls and a narrow work station.

'Just the whole thing. It was nice. I liked the way it felt.'

'They don't make places like that any more,' Tony said.

'They never did,' Graham said. 'They started to, but they didn't finish.'

'Still,' Kevo said, 'it feels like a shame it had to go.'

We'd rubbed out my own favourite that morning, in a dark corner away from the windows: a man at his desk, shoulders and feet square, a cup of coffee beside him, a briefcase by his feet. He was unremarkable in every way. He was just carrying on with his work. I'd felt a twinge as Graham applied the solvent and his head began to drip.

The office-building job was meant to be a week-long affair, but we got ahead of schedule. We worked hard all Thursday morning and packed it in by lunch, leaving the final floor, the top one, for the following day. I asked the lads not to tell anyone I'd let them go early, then spent the rest of the day walking around and drinking. I was restless for some reason. I hadn't been sleeping well. I kept thinking I saw someone I recognized in crowds or in the shadows.

On the side of a hotel on Amiens Street, I saw a figure that bore a striking resemblance to the ones painted in the office building. Like them he was faceless, like them he was thin and tall. He was obviously relaxing after a hard day. He wore his collar open, his tie loosened, and held his jacket over his shoulder. Where would he be going? I wondered. Home to a wife and kids? Or, like me, off aimlessly into the night? I decided that he did in fact work at our office building, and giggled at the thought of him and his co-workers clocking off when we did and heading out into their lives, bedding down for the night in their cosy homes and getting up earlier than us and beating us to the quays.

By seven o'clock, I'd crawled for miles between the pubs around the docks and over the river and back home to Irish-town. I had six or seven pints in me already by the time I pulled up a stool in the Oarsman. This was a classic pub, full of walnut wood and thick carpet and heavy optics and brass fittings. Over the course of my wanderings the cold had got in between my bones and skin, and something like nerves was making my mind feel scratchy. I added whiskeys to the pints for the sake of heating and anaesthetic and stayed in the pub until closing. Then I fell up the street, puked my ring in the bathroom sink and conked out with my cheek pressed against the cold tiles.

Friday morning I felt unsteady on the road. I scared myself with the way my hands shook on the wheel.

'Long night?' said Graham, climbing in. He looked a little worse for wear himself. His eyes were baggy, and he was wearing the same clothes he had worn the day before but now there were red blotches on his shirt and scuff marks on his knees.

Tony had brought coffees for everyone.

'You're a lifesaver,' Graham said.

'Just to mark my last day. Tomorrow I'm a free man.'

Tony's face was clear and open, his eyes bright. He was freshly shaven and had a new, clean haircut.

'Is that right?' Kevo said.

I looked at the docket. 'That's right.'

'Don't go easy on him now just 'cause he's nearly done,' Graham said. 'Work the bastard.' He sipped his coffee. 'This is grand though, Tone. Cheers.'

I drove us along the quay, with the windows open to air out my head. Glass buildings caught the light. Pedestrians jostled in the intersections drinking coffees from takeaway cups. And for a moment I felt as though we belonged among them, that we were part of a society, heading off to our jobs to make our humble contributions.

I parked the van and the lads hauled the equipment into the lobby. That vast, empty space swallowed the city's hustle and honk. The building felt embarrassed, like somehow we'd caught it off guard. We shouldered our bags and climbed the stairs, peering in at each landing to the open space and the walls we had cleaned. Just before the fourth-floor landing, we noticed a crumpled body painted on the stairs.

'Was that there before?' I said.

Kevo moved ahead. 'Someone's been in here,' he called back.

'Ah, for the love of fucking Jesus,' Tony said.

Graham pushed past me. 'Not much hope of you getting off lightly today, Tone.'

The branches of the potted plants by the windows now appeared broken. A litter of leaves and splintered wood had been added to the ground. The screens of desktop computers were smashed and their towers turned over. A printer lay on its side. Sheets of paper hung in the air. We looked into the faces of the office workers and saw new expressions of horror. The women were on their knees, hands up, begging. The men were frozen running or slumped against the walls. Bodies lay broken on the floor, their limbs folded at skewed angles. And everywhere there were messages, their letters scrawled and dripping. Help us, they said. Please, they said. Don't do this, they said. I turned and looked back the way we'd come and saw, painted on either side of the stairwell door, two masked men dressed all in black.

'Dear God,' Tony said. 'This is meant for us. What sick —'

'Anarchists,' Graham said, grinning.

'Christ,' Tony said, his eyes closed, 'will you ever just fucking shut up?'

Graham licked his lips and took a calm step forward. Tony was a solid guy — he'd been a rugby player in his student days — but I could tell that he was frightened. The look in Graham's eyes scared me too: it was not just that he wanted to inflict pain; he was eager to be hurt himself.

'Lads,' Kevo said, stepping between them. I helped him pull them apart and sent Tony to the other side of the floor.

'Careful,' I said, 'the both of you, or I'm writing you up.'

I listened to Tony's footsteps echo, and wanted desperately to leave, to make a run for the stairwell and to fall into a pub. Graham elbowed Kevo off and spat on the floor in Tony's direction. He picked up a bucket.

'Are we working or what?' he said.

Graham and Kevo started to scrub the walls. I suited up and helped them. We erased the furniture and the messages, the twisted faces, the groping hands. I held the ladder for Graham and took turns hosing the run-off with Kevo. We worked right through lunch with no talk and no radio, but at three o'clock Tony took it upon himself to go out for sandwiches. Graham accepted one soundlessly, and we ate them as we worked. We continued into the evening long after we were obliged to do so, and when the light began to fail I fetched torches from the van and we took turns holding them. It was nine o'clock by the time we'd finished and packed the van. We stood around outside, each of us wanting to leave but needing first to say or to hear something meaningful.

'Sorry about this morning,' Tony said.

'You will be,' Graham said, but there was nothing in it.

'Listen.' Tony looked at me from the tops of his eyes. 'Will you –'

'We'll say no more about it.'

I stood for a while and looked up and down the quays. The office blocks were dark but for the desk lamps of a handful of midnight-oilers. The river was high, black, and pulled with it a biting wind.

'But you two,' I turned to Graham and Kevo. 'I'll see you on Monday.'

I set off in the direction of human voices and found myself, some hours later, slumped on a high stool in a pub in Temple Bar, hating the expensive drink and the baseball caps for sale, the faded international currency pinned behind the bar, the dickhead playing Oasis covers over a jangling PA.

'We should all be ashamed of ourselves,' I said to no one in particular. I pointed myself in the direction of a greasy-haired manager who was leaning on the hatch talking to a floor girl. 'This place doesn't deserve to exist,' I said. 'It's a fucking fake.'

The manager frowned and puffed out his chest. The floor girl came shuffling over.

'You should go home,' she said.

In the ensuing months, I got flung out to Blanchardstown and Balbriggan and Clonskeagh and Kilcock. I'd drop the new lads off, head to the pub and come back for them five or six hours later. More than once, one of them had to drive us back to Dublin, and when they stopped showing up in the mornings I knew I couldn't report them.

One morning there was no one waiting at all and so, sick from drink, I drove to the assigned site, pulled on the overalls, poured the bitter chemicals and scrubbed away all day by myself. I drove back to town, dropped the van at the depot and walked home along Pearse Street studying my hands. The pigment I'd pulled from the wall had soaked into them and darkened. My skin was grey, its creases black at the knuckles. A mark like that of high tide scummed the balls of my wrists.

When I got to the Oarsman, I found Kevo behind the bar. I was surprised and happy to see him, though at first I didn't recognize him. He looked like a new man: cleanly shaven rather than stubbled; wearing a black shirt tucked into black trousers rather than overalls or jeans; and with his hair grown out, waxed and parted rather than shaved to the skull or hidden under a baseball cap.

'What are you doing here?' I said.

'Is this your local, is it? Just started last night.'

I ordered a drink and watched him pick a glass from the shelf, hold it at a perfect angle beneath the spout and pull the tap. The dark liquid crashed into the glass, rolled back on itself and rose. Kevo pushed back on the tap at the precise moment I would have done. He set the pint aside to settle and leaned across the bar. He smiled, and I realized how young he was, how possible it might be for him to do something. I asked about the other lads. He told me what he'd heard. That Graham finally had figured out how to hotwire a car, which he'd driven around for a night before slamming it into an eighteen-wheeler.

That Tony had some cockamamie plan to open up his own firm, but was still and probably forever would be working out the details.

PJ Nolan, incidentally, bought three restaurants from a bad bank for one euro apiece. The last I heard, he's doing reasonable business.

A Man Should Be Able to Do Things

The first time I tried to install the star nut, I had no soft blocks to cushion the dropouts and no vice to steady the fork, so I rigged up the front end and straddled the wheel, squeezing with my knees. I placed the nut in the mouth of the steering tube and covered it with a scrap of driftwood. I took a hammer from my father's toolbox, weighed it in my hand.

The shed was crammed with old paint cans and broken patio chairs and musty cardboard boxes spilling lawnmower engine parts. When he was younger, my father had used it as a workshop. On summer weekends, he'd patched punctures and replaced chain guards for Mona's friends and mine, and in winter he'd resealed hulls for small fishermen and varnished our mother's furniture. I'd grown up fascinated and enraged by the hours he chose to spend secluded from us in there. But since I'd returned to him, and found his bike corroding, I'd taken it on as a project and made the shed my own.

Already I'd stripped away the rusted components and cleaned a decade's worth of sand and grease from the frame. I'd raided the plastic boxes on the shelves for tools and inner tubes, and visited the bike shop in Balbriggan for a pair of chrome hubs, a brushed steel headset and stem, a set of aluminium brake levers and calipers and the most expensive chainset I could afford.

I swung the hammer and felt a nice shudder in my wrist, but when I lifted the wood the nut fell to the floor and rolled to rest by my heel. I set everything up and swung the hammer again but this time missed the centre of the wood and lodged the nut at an angle. When I tried to pry it out, it splintered in the hammer's claw. When I fished for it, I cut a red slice in the meat of my thumb. When I leaned the bike against the wall, the wheels slipped their stays and the frame and fork keeled over. I stood for a while with my thumb in my mouth and looked at what I'd done.

In the kitchen, the kettle whistled beside a bowl of oats and raisins. A cup with a tea bag scrunched inside sat waiting on the worktop. I took a roll of plaster from the first-aid box beneath the sink and bandaged my thumb, lifted the kettle from its cradle and made the porridge and the tea. I set a tray and climbed the stairs to the study, where I found my father hunched over his desk, still wearing his blue bathrobe and black gorilla-foot slippers.

The desktop was a salvaged ship door from Napoleonic times; years before, Dad had planed and sanded it and bolted it to driftwood legs. The shelves above his head held complete boxed sets of *Popular Mechanics*, *Civil Aircraft Markings*, *Propliner Magazine* and *Automotive Repair*, as well as his slide collection, his stamp collection and his library of films recorded from TV. I set the breakfast things down in front of him. He stared blankly at the cup and bowl, then stretched his right hand in the wedge of light that angled in from the high window. The fingers were surprisingly slender.

'You see that?' he said.

'See what?'

'That ring.'

'That's your wedding ring, Dad.'

His eyes were quick. 'Christ, I know *that*. You dirty-looking eejit. I'm not all gone yet that I'd forget a thing like *that*.'

His finger tapped the freckled hollow at his temple. He held out his other hand, the third finger of which showed a pale band of soft skin beneath the knuckle.

'But I usually wear it on *this* finger is the thing. I change it sometimes when I have to remind myself to do something, you know. Your mother taught me that, but . . . What was it, is what I want to know. Do you understand me? I've forgotten what it was I was supposed to remember.'

'It'll come back to you,' I said, as evenly as I could.

Before my second attempt at installing the star nut, I tuned the spokes, ran new tubes inside new tyres and bolted the wheels to the frame and fork. I greased the headset bearings and screwed on the compression rings. I magic-markered a red X in the centre of the scrap of wood and positioned it over the mouth of the steering tube. Then I raised the hammer, brought it down and felt a shudder and a little give. I repositioned the wood and brought the hammer down a second time. A third.

The wood slipped, and I knew before I looked that the nut had broken. When I did look, I saw a long fissure that my hammer alone could not have caused. It was the result of an original flaw, a weakness in the casting. I took a thin piece of sawn-off scrap metal and hammered the nut all the way through the hollow tube to the floor. I knew that I would have to take the bus to Balbriggan to get another one. But as I gathered up the pieces and flung them in the bin, I took solace from the knowledge that it was the nut, and not my method, that had been defective.

On my way to the bus, I offered to walk Dad to his doctor's appointment. We took the cycle path that hugged the dunes behind the house. The sky was low above a tidal plain dark with seaweed, the waves a deep icy blue where they broke on the near side of the island line. The arcade and the chip shop were shuttered for the season. Dad greeted the drunks huddled on the wall by the public toilets each by name. We cut through the lane by the caravan park and came out on the main street at the monument to Great War dead. At the surgery, I said goodbye but found myself unwilling to leave.

'Do you want me to come in with you?' I said.

'But you'll miss your bus then, won't you?'

'Yeah, but . . . You can get home all right?'

Dad looked past me up the street. In the near distance the red front door of the house was visible. He laughed.

'Fuck off, you,' he said.

The owner of the bike shop in Balbriggan had a high forehead and a cabled throat, oily fingernails and plastic glasses mended with electrical tape. Behind him was a corkboard to which faded posters from suppliers were pinned, in front of him a glass case strewn with so many parts it looked as though a bike had exploded in there.

He wanted to talk about the merits of the new Shimano range and about his sons' successes in the downhill racing leagues. I rushed the transaction as politely as possible, half-ran for the return bus and stood up front by the driver watching the rocks of the coastline blurring past the window.

Back at home, I walked from room to room looking for Dad. His bowl of porridge and his cup of tea were still upstairs, untouched. As I cleaned them at the sink, I told myself that he must be stuck in the usual queue behind wheezing smokers and diabetic fatsos. Or maybe he had gone to the bookies for a flutter or ducked into the Lifeboat for a pint.

I went to the front door, opened it. As I searched the empty street in both directions, my phone rang: Mona.

'How's Dad?'

'He's fine,' I said.

'Can I speak to him?'

Her voice was sleepy, the background loud with RTÉ radio and the sound of Colm and the kids laughing together.

'Not right now,' I said. 'I'm not sure where he is.'

I could imagine my sister's eyes shimmering the way they did whenever anger started to boil. Her top lip, I knew, was clamped between her teeth and her ears moved as she worked her jaw, the skin stretched tight at the corners of her eyes.

The third time I tried to install the star nut, I took the nut from the bag and laid it in the mouth of the steering tube, covered it with the scrap of wood and brought the hammer down. The nut went in first time. I slid a half-inch spacer over the end of the tube and bolted the stem in place, turned the Allen bolt in the top cap until I felt it catch and swivelled the stem from side to side. I lifted the front end, bounced the tyre off the ground and tried to rock the headset but it wouldn't budge.

I bolted the handlebars to the stem, slipped on the brake levers and gear shifters and secured them all in place, greased the ends of the handlebars and slid on a new set of rubber grips, greased the bearings and threaded the axle and screwed in the bracket cups, screwed the pedals to the crankset and bolted that to the axle, hung the derailleurs, attached the new chain, hung the brake calipers and set the pads and ran all the cables through their sheaths, bolted the saddle to the seat post and coaxed that into the frame, screwed on mudguards and reflectors and a headlamp and a rear blinker.

I wheeled the bike out of the shed and climbed into the saddle. I pushed off, rolled to the back gate and slid back the bolt. A dog trotting on the cycle path inclined its head and watched me. The wind whistled through the dune grass. I didn't move.

Through the living-room window, I watched the sky threaten rain. I turned on the TV and flipped between people making over their houses or faces. I made a cup of tea and let it go cold, peeled back the bandage to see how my thumb was healing. I ached for a cigarette. I missed my mother.

I heard the front door click, heard the scratch of Dad's shoes on the doormat. I was up from the couch and standing next to him before he knew it.

'You gave me a fright,' he said, unwinding his scarf from his neck. 'You'll never guess who I ran into. Remember Noely Caldwell? The old fishmonger? He's not been well, God bless him. Something with his heart.'

'Where the hell have you been?'

Dad frowned innocently and offered a red plastic shopping bag.

'I was talking to Noely. In his shop. I got us dinner.'

I left him in the hall and went to the kitchen to call Mona

back. She was on her way out to me, she said, her voice levelled to a flat calm.

'It's okay,' I told her. 'He's just got in the door.'

Mona's voice shuddered and she and Colm began exchanging muffled words. I waited.

'Look,' she said, 'we're coming down tomorrow. We need
to talk to both of you. It's just . . . I need to talk to both of you.'

Dad took a paper parcel from the bag and unwrapped it by
the sink to reveal a silver fish. He took a wooden cutting board
from the cabinet and a shining cleaver from the block.

'Don't!' I said, a little too loudly.

'What?' Mona said. 'What's happening?'

I cupped my hand over the mouthpiece.

'I'll do that in a minute,' I told Dad, who dropped the cleaver
and threw up his hands and stalked out into the garden. I stared
at the door for a moment.

'What?' Mona said. 'What is it?'

'He was trying . . .' I said. 'I overreacted. He was about to
butcher a fish.'

I could hear Mona's kids again in the background and Colm
closing cupboards. I kneaded my forehead against the pain
behind my eyes and discovered that my hand was trembling.

'Look,' Mona said, 'you've been very good to him. I just
think that maybe now's the time to move him. I'm sorry. I'm
just so worried and so frazzled and I can't –'

'Easy, Mo,' I said. 'We're all right. We'll figure it out.'

'I'm glad it's you out there and not me. Does that make me a terrible person?'

Through the kitchen window, I could see the light go on in the shed and Dad's silhouette moving about in there.

I washed, peeled, sliced potatoes and dropped them into a pot of water to boil. I scraped the fish's scales, broke sprigs of dill and thyme from the herb box and chopped them, picked a lemon from the fruit bowl and cut it into discs, took salt and pepper from the spice rack and stuffed the wet pink cavity until the fish bulged at the gills. I laid it on a roasting tray and slid it into the oven.

Outside it was dark already. From beyond the back wall, I could hear the sea rolling, and through the shed window, I could see Dad standing beside the bike, one hand resting on its handlebars. As I walked the garden path, I felt moisture from bent-over grass fronds soak the ends of my jeans. I resolved to mow the lawn in the morning, unless the rain came back. I shouldered the sticking door and stepped into the shed.

'This is my bike,' Dad said.

He had taken off his jacket and flung it in a dusty corner. His shirtsleeves were rolled up, his top button undone to show the fraying neckline of a white vest.

'How was the doctor?' I said.

'But you rebuilt it.'

Dad tried to rock the headset.

'Yes,' I said. 'I did.'

'Good. That's good. You might have a talent for this, you know? And that'll stand to you. A man should be able to do things.'

Dad flipped the bike over and rested it on its saddle and handlebars.

'I've been working on something inside myself I'll show you later on,' he said. 'But it's a surprise for your mother, now, so don't go telling your sister. She can't keep a secret, that girl.'

He turned a pedal, pressed the shifter and grinned as the chain moved smoothly up and down the gears.

'Good. That's good,' he said. 'But she looks up to you, you know. When she starts in school you should take care of her.'

Dad's shoulder blades flared through his shirt as he turned the bike over and laid it on its tyres.

'Look,' he said, a bead of sweat forming in the crease of his lip. 'I know you don't know what I'm on about now. But you'll understand me when you're older.'

Dad's hand moved along the crossbar to the saddle. I took a step towards him, then a step back.

Everything

Dark clouds had followed us from Dublin to central Meath. When finally they broke on Saturday morning, neighbours telephoned Melissa's parents with news of flooding. In the early gloaming, Ciarán and I hauled sandbags to the milking shed, and then, while he spun the Land Rover into town, Melissa and I ate a three-hour lunch with Siobhán and covered invites, footwear, cake.

'We'd better be leaving early tomorrow if we're going to get yous home,' Ciarán said that night over dinner (boutonnières, placecards, flower girls' dresses).

But on Sunday morning there was a break in the rain. I sat on the edge of the bed to tie my trainers. Melissa yawned and rolled over, baring a white shoulder. The sheets caught in the crook of her knee and tautened against her back. I bent to place a kiss at her ear and at once I felt cunning and ashamed: what I'd really wanted, when I'd packed my running gear for the weekend, was to ensure some time alone.

A bank of swollen cloud loomed over the puddled driveway.

The wind had stilled and the countryside was eager and delirious. Above the blackberry bushes a swarm of greenflies hummed a crazy music. A flock of starlings burst from the telephone line and squawked at nothing. A narrow road took me under a canopy of dripping trees, to the crest of a brief hill and down into a flooded gully. I came to a stile and looked beyond it: rolling, quiet gold. I clambered over. Tongues of corn applied their slaver to my shins.

Melissa was waiting for me in the hallway at the foot of the staircase, wearing only the mock-Victorian nightgown I'd bought for her the previous Christmas. Its hanging collar framed a hard nub of breastbone; its tail hit just above the jagged scar sunk into her left thigh – mark of a refusing mare and of a shattered femur that ached still whenever the barometer dropped.

'They're away at Mass, you know,' she said, narrowing her eyes.

'Are they, now?' I said.

I watched Melissa climb the stairs, and for a moment – the fall of her feet, the flex of her calves – it was as though I were nineteen again and back in the fusty hallway of her Rathmines digs. My hands were sweating, I realized, not from the run but from her, as they had done back then – so much so, once, that I'd dropped the cheap bottle of red wine I'd spent half an hour selecting.

In the bedroom I found her naked, the nightdress flung on the floor. She stood in front of the full-length mirror squeezing the flesh at her ribs. I struggled out of my gear and crept across the room, but when Melissa felt me against her back she tensed.

'Shower first,' she said. 'You stink.'

I reached my hands around her waist.

'I thought you liked my stink.'

'That's disgusting,' she laughed. 'When did I say a thing like that?'

'Before.'

'Before! Before, I pretended to like a lot of things – before I knew better!'

'Like what?'

'Your singing.'

'What else?'

'Your *dancing*!'

'Be honest, now, you like my dancing.' And I danced, flesh slopping back and forth on its loose tethers to my bones.

Melissa turned and laid her hands on my chest. Her hair smelled of fruit.

'I liked it in a boyfriend.' She bit the corner of a smile. 'But my husband will have to be a better dancer.'

'Oh, really?' I fumbled for her hips but she skittered away from me and disappeared into the wardrobe crammed with her teenage clothes. I planted my bare arse on her desk. 'Well, then, maybe I'm just not husband material after all.'

'If you say you're not, you're not.' I heard the click of many hangers. 'But I'll tell you one thing: you'd better not embarrass me for our first dance.'

'And if I do?'

'Then I'll be forced to get a divorce.'

'On what grounds?'

'Clumsiness.'

'"Your honour, I can no longer in good conscience remain married to this man, for he is clumsy"?'

'Exactly.'

'Seems a bit extreme.'

'It is what it is.'

Melissa emerged from the wardrobe holding in each hand a blue polka-dot party frock, nearly identical. She laid them both on the bed and turned to finger through the necklaces arranged on hooks in her travelling jewellery box. Her hand moved quickly, stopped, and rose to rub the notches at the base of her neck.

'Have you seen my little Claddagh earrings?'

'No,' I sighed. 'But I'm sure they'll turn up. We'll look for them after.'

'After?' In her eyes there was a glimmer of gleeful cruelty. 'After what now, exactly?'

Whenever I stayed at Melissa's parents' house, I liked to take long showers in the screened, claw-footed tub. Then I'd sit on the toilet, leaf through the copies of *Old Moore's Almanac* arranged on the cistern and study their alien world of weather lore and sheep dip. I rooted through the medicine cabinet to check the progress of Siobhán's anxiety treatment, cracked the frosted window and looked out over moving fields. The sky above them was murderous but the fields were reconciled and quiet. I leaned my elbows on the window sill and endured for as long as I could.

The air in the kitchen was sharp with the tang of bleach and the tiles were tacky underfoot. Melissa's eyes were riveted to the screen of the wall-mounted TV, where a grave-faced meteorologist laid hands on the country's centre. At the opposite end of the room, Siobhán busied herself unloading things from shopping bags. The bite marks of elastic across her stomach made her look as though she'd been assembled in a hurry.

'Need a hand, there?' I asked and Melissa turned on me, her tongue a spike between crooked teeth.

'No, you're grand,' Siobhán said.

Rain resumed its beat against the kitchen window. Water bubbled at the base of the sliding door. Outside, beneath the eaves of the milking shed, a herd of sheltering cattle moaned.

'Squalling out there, ha Mel?' Siobhán said, stacking beans on top of peas on top of corn.

Melissa studied the television.

'Looks like,' I said.

'Melissa.' Siobhán could not be deterred. 'I forgot to tell you who I ran into – only Mary McConvey of all people. Has a voucher for glycolic peels over at Alchemy that Christy gave her for her birthday – subtlety, as ever, not exactly being Christy's strong suit. Face on her of recent, to be honest, like a bumpy road. Herself and myself are considering one before the wedding. Interested?'

'So, she's coming too?'

Siobhán finished her task in silence. When everything was put away she made a beeline for me, took my stubbled jaw in her hand as she strode past and said:

'You'll do.'

I gathered breakfast things from the cupboards and seated myself beside Melissa. When I reached for the white plastic flower she'd pinned to the side of her head, she recoiled, her face pinched.

'I'm not in the mood,' she said.

What had happened, I knew, was what always happened: Melissa had fought with her mother out of fear and frustrated love. She wanted the reception to be elegant and intimate; Siobhán wanted to invite a mob of family and friends.

My head slid into my hands. The pulse in my thumb met that in my temple.

'Okay, look,' I said, 'I mean, they *are* paying . . . Would it really be the end of the world –'

'Stop defending her! You're supposed to be on my side.

When we're married you'll have to agree with me in everything, even when I'm wrong.'

I could see the full circumference of Melissa's blue irises, the whites around them glaring.

'Why even when you're wrong?'

'Because if I'm wrong then who the hell else is going to agree with me?' She covered her face with her hands and mumbled, 'Oh, maybe we shouldn't be doing this. Maybe this is all just a huge mistake. Maybe you're not ready.'

I laid my hand between her warm shoulder blades.

'Hey, hey, Mel,' I said, 'of course we should, you know we should. I agree with you, okay? And I'll talk to your mother, okay?'

'You don't understand.' Melissa's voice had emptied out. 'It's none of those things. It's everything.'

'What do you mean everything?'

'I mean everything.'

I took my hand from Melissa's back and spooned a nugget of cereal towards my face.

Ciarán leaned over the banister and shouted, 'Are we right there so, are we?' He crossed his arms and frowned, lips rehearsing the shapes of words.

'So, come here to me, so,' he said, sidling closer but with his gaze still fixed on the banister's carved volute. 'Have you given any more thought to what we talked about the other night?'

'Look,' I said. 'I'm really grateful. I'm sure we both are but –'

'Say no more. You have your pride. You're an eejit but I can understand that.'

Ciarán bent to inspect a flake of varnish. I watched him work it with a nail and thought about the smells of a thousand dinners breathing from the house's pores. Siobhán appeared on the landing, tottering in heels.

'Here's Miss Ireland, now,' Ciarán said.

'He's terrible,' Siobhán beamed.

Melissa followed, wearing now, I thought, the other polka-dot dress. I felt the urgency of a hair's sweep, of a tooth-print on a lip – mark of sadness. Ciarán dug a hand into his jacket pocket and Melissa smiled when she saw what he offered.

'Just cleaning out the car,' Ciarán said as she affixed the earrings. 'Came across them.'

Blasts of wind shook the trees and tore at the bushes. A hungry pool of water swallowed the drops that slashed its face.

'Brollies,' Ciarán said and took two golf umbrellas from the stand by the door. 'Bring the car around, son?'

'Very funny,' I said.

'I just can't understand it,' Siobhán said. 'How does someone get by at your age having never learned to drive?'

'City boy.' I lifted our bags. 'Never the need, I suppose.'

'Suburban boy.' Siobhán sucked her teeth. 'Your mother.'

'Will you leave him alone,' Ciarán told her as we braved the driveway. 'Sure, there'll be need enough soon enough when the children start arriving.'

The Land Rover was cold, its carpets spotless. I squeaked close to Melissa on the leather seat but she leaned away from me. Siobhán and Ciarán bundled in and Ciarán set the wipers fighting.

'My Christ,' he said. 'Have you ever seen anything like this? We'll be rounding up the animals two by two in a minute.'

The Land Rover jolted over the cattle grid and sloshed to the centre of town. Cars stood abandoned by the kerb at hasty angles. Old women and teenagers avoided each other beneath the Pricebuster's awning. We revolved slowly at a roundabout and slipped on to a ramp for the dual carriageway. I peered out through the windscreen and the rain and saw two lines of slow red lights.

'I know what we can do to pass the time,' Ciarán said. 'Why don't we play a little game?'

'Because, Dad, that'd be tedious.'

'Well, what better ideas do you have?'

'Turn on the radio,' Siobhán said.

Ciarán tuned through static to a wall of hysterical pop, against which Siobhán objected; then on to a murmur of lachrymose country, against which Melissa did. He found a GAA match report: Siobhán and Melissa groaned in unison.

'Well, then.' Ciarán snapped the radio off. 'If that's going to be your attitude then we can just sit here in silence.'

Melissa's legs were crossed and she was staring straight ahead, eyes fixed, jaw set. What was her expression?

'All right, Mel?' I said. 'Are you warm enough, there?'

'Fierce weather altogether,' Ciarán said. 'Fierce.'

I wiped my window and looked out at heavy branches tilting over a rusted guiderail. A single shoe scudded by on the current. I groped in the footwell for my umbrella.

'I think I'll get out,' I said, 'and go see what the problem is.'

'Good man, yourself,' Siobhán said.

'Are you serious? You'll be drownded.' Ciarán swivelled in his seat. 'Will you stop him, Melissa?'

'He's free to do what he wants.'

The sky twisted grey into black, and thundered. Water surged in the ditch beyond the shoulder and the trees and hedges shook. Would we ever make it back to Dublin? And if we did, would Melissa stay angry with me all the way? In front of her parents? What *was* her expression?

The umbrella made little difference: rain seeped into my shoes and trousers and found its way to the corners of my eyes. I pushed on, squinting in through fogged windows at bouncing children and stone-eyed parents. Engines ticked away frustrated. Headlights lit the rain. At the head of the jam, at a dip in the road, a pond had formed across all four lanes. Traffic moving in the opposite direction slowed and waded through, but the pond was deeper on our side. In the fast lane a van sat spluttering. In the slow lane a Mercedes hunkered, dark and vacant. A man and two children stood marooned nearby.

The man hopped and waved. Was he calling for me? I picked my way towards him through the tangle of clamouring bonnets.

'Hey.' The man had to shout above the rain. 'Hey, I need some help.' His shoulders were stooped from cold or worry but his clothes promised a comfortable room in which later to discuss all this. 'I have to get back to the car and fetch my phone. We bailed out when the water started coming in the doors and I forgot it. Can you watch these two for just a minute? Please.'

The children gawped up at me. They both wore scarlet raincoats. The little girl's nostrils were muzzled in snot. The little boy's teeth were tiny.

'This is Gráinne,' the man said. 'And this is Michael.'

Michael lunged for me and took me by the hand. His skin was soft but through it his bones felt oddly strong. Gráinne edged closer and installed a finger in a nostril. I angled my umbrella over the children's heads. Behind us car horns honked a low lament and somewhere an aeroplane added its whine to the sizzle and gurgle. The man waded into the water, knees high, arms spread. My arm jerked as Michael dropped into a series of high-energy squat thrusts. The man reached the car, hauled its passenger door open and ducked inside. Michael rose and fired a toe deep into his sister's shin. An anguished vowel escaped her lips and she buckled but didn't fall. The torturer resumed his calisthenics. Gráinne pressed her face against my hip.

The man waded back holding his phone aloft in triumph. He ignored the children – one sobbing, one smirking.

'Thanks a lot,' he said.

'You're grand,' I said. 'But you should know that Michael –'

'Thanks a lot,' the man said again.

He dialled a number and raised the rescued phone to his ear. Michael waved a manic goodbye and Gráinne crept up behind her brother, wrapped her ankle around his and shoved. The boy fell on his face with a splash and a hollow pop.

'Jesus!' The man dropped to his hunkers.

I backed away and put the width of a bonnet between us. Michael writhed in the water. Gráinne tucked a strand of hair behind her ear and bent to help her brother to his feet. The man returned to his phone.

I traipsed back along the length of the jam and looked again through windows. Brows were furrowed, knuckles strained. The furious and the panicked were pulling U-ies in the reservation. Beyond the seething treeline, the fields accepted water.

After a while I found the Land Rover. Through the windscreen I could see Ciarán gazing into his lap and Siobhán staring straight ahead. Between them I could make out a sliver of Melissa's shoulder.

I looked back towards the trees. Their leaves fitted together, shook apart, rejoined.

I thought about running.

I didn't run.

Strong

The new armoires will arrive on Wednesday morning, but the truck to take the old ones away can't make it until Thursday afternoon. Randy, the general manager, and Agnes, the head of housekeeping, call Luis and me into the back office first thing Monday to figure out a plan.

Randy wears contrast shirts with a rim of grease at collar and cuff. Agnes has a thatch of orange hair that rasps against her boxy shoulder pads. As they deliberate, Luis stares into his hands, chin lolling on the chest of a brown polyester shirt three sizes bigger than mine. And when Agnes decides that the two of us should hump four floors' worth of oversized mock-rococo armoires to the roof and cram them beneath the patio canopy, Luis ignores her, nods at Randy and says:

'Yes, boss.'

But in the elevator it's a different story.

'Goddamn it,' he says, 'have you seen those motherfuckers? They're six feet tall and three wide. They're two hundred fucking pounds.' He drives a boot into the base of the panelled door; the elevator jolts on its cable. 'Man, it wouldn't take too much more to make me hate this place, you know? I mean, really hate it. All we ever do is fix it up, but it's still a dump. Why don't they just bulldoze it all to hell and start again?'

'It's an institution,' I tell him, but I'm distracted with my phone: no calls.

The hotel, according to Randy, dates back to the beginning of the last century. Its first customers were the owners of the lumberyards upriver, whose patronage paid for canopied beds and brick hearths tall enough to stand in, whose sons held lavish dinners throughout Prohibition behind the laundry room's trick door. During the Second World War, naval officers billeted at the university marched down North King Street three times daily for meals in the tavern. Postwar, travelling salesmen staged product demonstrations in their rooms until the yards all closed and there was no one left to sell to.

It was to the hotel's restaurant that I took my parents for cobb salads and whiskey sours on the weekend of freshman orientation. My mother wore a purple sweater and waterproof eye make-up, my father a ludicrous white linen jacket and a wide smile. And it was there too that I took Ashley two years later for thick steaks and strong cocktails after exams I knew I'd failed. I held her hand tightly across the table, listened to her talk about our future. Her voice was high and she could hardly sit still. That was before our sex got angry, our conversations short.

Now, I'm awake most mornings before my alarm and staring at the plastic stars constellated on Luis's living-room ceiling. I fold the *Star Wars* blanket marked with his childhood piss and work the coffee-maker that dominates the countertop in the kitchenette. Then we're in the car, Luis slurping coffee from a travel mug and singing along to the country station, or the oldies station. We pull into the parking lot and punch our time cards at the door. We nod hello to the cleaning ladies hollering down their phones and to the overnight room-service guys comparing tips. And then we're in the elevator, on the floors, in the rooms, changing light bulbs or mopping tiles or rewiring the busted cable. Luis and I work well together. We are capable of talking about nothing to pass the time. But the major advantage of our kind of work is the opportunity it provides for silence.

The old armoires are cheap plywood boxes with particle-board backs and doors of imitation oak. I've gotten used to fielding complaints from guests about sticking drawers or misaligned hinges or splintered innards that shred cashmere sweaters. I lower them one by one on to a hand truck. Luis steers and I hold them steady. We ride the elevator to the roof, where, this past summer, we used to sneak away for smokes and feel the sun dry the sweat from our backs. But it's winter now, the air is as sharp as teeth and everything is the same iron grey as the sky. Luis and I collapse the patio chairs and unload the armoires beneath the canopy. I survey the space.

'Will they all fit?'

He shrugs. 'That's not my problem.'

To look at him, you'd think Luis was strong. When we met on my first day, I looked up into his black little piggy eyes and fist of a mouth, then down at the neckless spread of him, and I was scared. But these past few months, since he's taken me in and we've started to share a bathroom, I've seen the slushy hang of what I'd thought were biceps, the slabs of meat swinging from his chest, the slender legs.

By mid-morning, he's sweated through two shirts and needs to take a break every few minutes to catch his breath. It gets so bad that, after lunch, I fetch him a Gatorade from the vending machine and leave him wheezing in the stairwell. The only way to preserve the armoires' joints is to get right under their tilting weight, and if I wedge the hand truck against a wall the work is just about doable alone. By four o'clock, I've moved nineteen of the things to the roof and stacked them end to end. That's almost half the job, and the rest will fit if we disassemble the last couple and lay them in pieces on top.

While the sun fizzles behind the flat roof of the old brewery, Luis and I sit together by the stairwell door to smoke. He flips through a porno he's found stashed behind some paint cans, jabbing at airbrushed flesh with every turn of the page. Randy comes to check on us, tie loosened to give rolling room to a beefy neck.

'That's nice work,' he says, and Luis is quick to tell him:

'You know us, boss.'

My parents met Ashley a couple of times. My father liked her sundress and the way she touched his arm. He reckoned that her watch and her haircut meant she came from money. My mother never liked her. Not when Ashley and I invited the two of them for dinner to the studio apartment off campus we'd decided to share for sophomore year. And definitely not when I made the call nine months later to declare that I was neither going back to school nor coming home, but instead would stay on to work while Ashley finished studying.

After that, my mother and I didn't speak for almost a month. My father called me Thursday evenings on his way back from after-work drunk bowling to tell me over and over that he didn't agree with my decision but he respected it, that my student loans were absolutely my problem and that my mother would come around. Eventually, he brokered a truce, and now my mother and I talk on the phone every week or two. She's stopped asking me to come home. She seldom asks me about work. She never asks me about Ashley; I haven't told her we broke up.

After our shift, Luis and I decide to head over to the Howling Owl, an off-brand Hooters by the railway tracks. He likes to sit at the belly of the horseshoe bar and pant as waitresses strut past gripping pitchers of weak beer. Me, I like the sports. The Owl has a bank of TVs near its copper ceiling that show everything from college football to ladies' synchronized diving. I can lock into the athletes' mechanical action, with Luis distracted and good company for it, and the crowd around us loud enough that I don't have to think. The hours fly by.

The record at the Owl on dollar wing night is fifty-one dollars, fifty-one wings. If you can beat that, your whole party eats and drinks for free, and they give you a T-shirt with a picture of an owl dripping buffalo sauce from its feathers, which Luis has been eyeing for months. He's been in training, conditioning his stomach. Last week, he broke forty for the first time and tonight he's feeling lucky.

When we arrive, the Owl is rocking already – Steve Miller Band and Big 10 basketball. We take our usual seats, order a pitcher, and Luis sets to jawing with some tattooed townie about last year's hockey play-offs and about why he doesn't vote. A bachelorette party slams tequilas at my elbow. The pitcher disappears before half-time. Luis manages just twenty-seven wings. We order a second pitcher, a third, and at last call Luis persuades one of the waitresses to slip us a bottle of gin for cash in hand.

He is too drunk to drive so I take the wheel and pilot us without thinking to our summer after-hours drinking spot upriver. The night is too cold for us to be here, and black but for our headlights. The air smells of frost and skunk. I sit shivering on the fender and Luis sprawls out flat on the hood. The ticking engine warms us as we pass the bottle back and forth.

I take out my phone to call Ashley. She doesn't answer. I leave a message.

'You shouldn't've done that,' Luis says. He is silent for a long time, looks disappointed. Eventually he says, 'And you've been on my couch for long enough.'

He rolls off the hood and staggers to the riverbank. For a moment, I'm worried and half-excited that he'll tumble over the edge but he steadies himself against a tree. I hear the slap of vomit on water, the shudder of dry heaves. He walks back, drawing a hand across his lips, and clambers into the car.

'Just fix it with Ashley,' he says. 'Okay? You only get so many chances.'

His big head thuds against the bulkhead. I drive us home with the window open to air the stink of vomit. I hope for a deer or a raccoon to appear in my high beams, something warm and alive that I could fail to avoid. But nothing comes.

In the morning, a voicemail from Ashley awaits me. She, as far as I know, still gets up at five a.m. to read, and right now she'll be on her way to her work-study at the gallery. How *fine* it was, she says, to hear from me, and behind her voice I can hear the weatherman forecast a blizzard on the TV I wired into our kitchen.

I work the coffee-maker, go out to smoke but keep walking, and find myself some time later zipping my jacket over my uniform and jogging through an iron gateway at the university's western end. At this hour, the campus is quiet: just some men from the phone company, an administrator type in a cherry-red Gore-Tex and a girl with an enormous backpack limping towards the library. Above me are the dorms, churchy grey stone piles with red-brick edging; and to the right is the concert auditorium, all swooping lines and hammered aluminium and vinyl posters of cellists. Before I flunked out I hardly ever went to class, but now I realize with a pang how long it's been since I've learned anything. I'd like to know how something works, why something is the way it is.

'Where the hell were you this morning?' Luis says in the locker room. He is freshly showered but his eyes are cloudy, clean-shaven but there are nicks in his tubby jaw.

I splash water on my face at the sink and smooth the hair at the nape of my neck.

'I went for a walk,' I tell him. 'Ashley left a message.'

'Oh.' Luis checks his watch; we collect the hand truck and head for the elevators. 'Man, I don't expect she was too happy. I couldn't believe it last night when you said what you said to her.'

'Well, there's no taking back any of it now.'

The doors open on a wobbly old guy wearing an Air Force

cap and oxygen tubes. Luis pushes the lobby button for him and leads us down the hallway to our first room. I put the strength of my shoulder hard into the armoire. All morning I shove and heave and blat the things on to the truck or into the carpet. At lunch we choke down plates of sodden calamari left over from a Chamber of Commerce meeting.

After lunch, I steady the hand truck, pin it down with a forearm when the armoire tries to tip it. Above me, more than my own weight in wood teeters and groans, and the only sign of Luis is the squeak of his hands on the veneer. I dive out of the way. The floorboards shake, the crash fills the room but the joints hold firm. Agnes, on one of her rounds, peers around the door frame and levels her grey eyes at us.

'Sorry,' Luis says, his cheeks flushed with hatred. 'I slipped.'

'Is that right?'

'That's right,' I tell her.

'Well, don't slip again.'

'No, Agnes,' Luis says.

We take the armoire to the roof to break it apart. Luis kicks like a horse but I'm all frantic hands, tearing at joints and punching twisted laths and snapping pieces of particle board until my nail beds sting with splinters. The wind has picked up and the canopy fills. It flutters empty and fills again.

The air reaches around my waist where my shirt tail hangs and down the back of my neck where my jacket collar gapes; it numbs my lips and scrapes my throat and freezes my breath in fog. I pass the Chinese restaurant and the yoghurt place full of hollering upperclassmen, the cocktail bar where Randy goes to pretend he is somewhere else.

The main road out of town has no crosswalk; I take the stone steps to an underpass lit with the flicker of a trashcan fire. Around it circle two men swaddled in overcoats and one bare-legged and shivering in a dirty hospital gown. The tunnel roof dribbles the condensation of human breath.

I climb out again at the warehouse district where, at a raw space on the corner, an exhibition opening leaks its chatter on to the sidewalk. The warehouse I'm aiming for is in the middle of the block; it is built of brown brick, single-storeyed but with lofted ceilings and tall plate windows in which a chill moon dangles. I get out of the street light and smoke some cigarettes, careful to cup my hand over the embers. In dark corners and in the coldest places, the snow has begun to stick.

When the lights go off, I cross the street to meet her as she closes up. I watch the delicate way she balances a fat bag on a shoulder and a box of files against a knee.

'You could've come in,' she says without turning. She turns a key; the shutters rattle down.

'I got your message,' I say and offer a hand to help her down the steps but she doesn't need it.

Her ponytail has been severed, leaving a straight-edged bob.

Her thin cheeks blanch from the chill and her small nose reddens; I want to cup the heat of my hands around her ears.

'I'm sorry,' I tell her.

She shrugs. 'I'm used to it.'

The party on the corner disgorges middle-aged couples. They wear camel-hair coats and broad-brimmed hats and clog the sidewalk to air-kiss. Ashley pops the trunk and I help her load her things. Her smell is old coffee and new perfume.

'You look good,' I say.

She crosses her arms and screws her lips into the goofy appraiser's face she used to practise in front of the bathroom mirror.

'You look . . .' she says, 'the same. In fact, I think you're wearing the same exact outfit as the last time I saw you.'

'It's a uniform.' I tug at the knees of my pants. 'You've cut your hair.'

'It was time for a change.'

'It makes you look strong.'

She smiles. 'That's exactly what I wanted.'

'And you're happy?' I say. 'You're doing good work?'

'I am. I really am.'

I notice gobs of snow settled on my boot and kick them off.

'That's good, Ashley,' I say. 'That's really good.'

For a short time in the eighties, when business was at its worst, the hotel opened its fourth floor to residential rentals. The

people who took them mostly were short-term stays: professors with a one-semester contract or the better-off students
between dorms for the summer months. There were some
older people too who, once their children had left and their
husbands or wives passed on, sold or rented their big Colonials
to free up cash and to be in town.

Mrs Kimmel made the move in her late sixties and was surprised to live for another twenty-five years. She took out her
disappointment at still being alive on whomever she could,
insisted that the cleaning staff was stealing from her and called
Luis 'Taco' until he told her that was Mexican, then did her
research and called him 'Ajiaco' instead. One of my first jobs at
the hotel was cleaning out her suite after she died. There were
just a few items of over-laundered clothing and some old
room-service plates – no books, no photos of anyone. But it
wasn't the modesty or even the loneliness of her life that made
an impression on me; it was how, throughout those years as her
mind gave up, her body had persisted, kept moving air and
blood.

I think of Mrs Kimmel as I sneak in through the staff entrance
and take the stairs to the banqueting floor; as I peek into the
restaurant and find it dark, cross the room and lie down behind
the polished warming stations. I used to think that if my body
had even half her kind of resilience, I would be okay. But as I lay
my head on a folded tablecloth and curl beneath another one,
I'm not so sure.

All night, the floorboards creak, branches scratch the windowpanes and the elevator cables whir. From time to time, the night porter comes and sits at the table by the big bay window to pick over stolen French fries. I hold my breath, stay perfectly still, and when he is gone I take out my phone to watch a short video I recorded a little over a year ago before everything went to hell. In it, Ashley stands in our kitchen swamped in one of my sweatshirts. She is cooking to the Supremes, her small knees bouncing. She spoons something red and steaming from a pot and offers it to the camera.

I wake before the breakfast service and sneak back out the staff entrance. Overnight, the snow has come on heavy and now it lies in deep drifts over the parking lot. I wade downtown and back for coffee and sit with it in the locker room until Luis comes in looking rumpled. He takes his coffee without a word and leads us to the lobby to await the new armoires' arrival. Outside, city ploughs struggle to clear and salt the way.

The truck rounds the corner and skids to a halt at the forecourt. Its tyres crunch and its lights blink as Luis backs it in to the goods entrance. The deliverymen, Baptiste and Kenny, have an invoice for Agnes to sign.

'This is a nice hotel,' says Baptiste, whose sinewy arms are bare even in this weather.

'Real nice,' Kenny says and whistles through a gap in his teeth.

The new armoires are built of marbled walnut and intricately carved, with brass inlays and smooth-running drawers and recessed rails for hangers. They are heavier than the old ones and their joints are more secure. Baptiste and Kenny take half and Luis and I take half. Randy joins us midway through the morning and rolls up his greasy sleeves.

Once the new armoires have all been put in place, Agnes gives Baptiste and Kenny her best directions back to the highway; and Randy, Luis and I take the elevator to the roof to think over how we'll dispose of the old ones tomorrow. As we rise, I hope that the canopy legs have snapped overnight from the weight of snow. I picture half a foot's accumulation hugging the shapes of the broken and the whole alike. But when the doors open, I see that all is as we left it. The canopy sags, its legs buckle and bend – but it holds strong yet. And beneath it the armoires wait, clean and cold to the touch. Randy takes a broom from the stairwell and jabs it into the canopy's belly. Hunks of snow fly skyward and break apart and float in dust to the street below.

There will be no fresh starts for me, I realize. But there will be starts.

How to Go Home

Open your eyes. Unclench your teeth. Relax your grip on the armrest. Take your iPod and your bad novel from the seat pocket in front of you. Queue in the aisle. Smile at the air hostess. Make eye contact. Say thanks.

Feel the damp air test your lungs as you step out on to the jetway. Resist the urge to punch the Yorkshireman with the meaty neck who dawdles in your path and is complaining already to his tiny wife about mobile phone reception. Take the stairs, traipse the corridors, follow the signs. Be patient.

Hurry through baggage collection and out into Arrivals, past the crowd of faces all disappointed at the sight of you. Head outside for the taxi rank. It's cold but brilliantly bright and for a moment you're blinded but then your vision clears and you can see that the place is just as you left it.

Direct the taxi driver past the cricket club and under the railway bridge, this way around the roundabout, that way at the crossroads. Watch the old man who laid your mother's patio limp along in step with his dog, and two women – friends of your mother's – stoop to admire the Council flower beds.

Arrive at your estate. Pay the taxi driver and stand for a moment to savour two rows of identical white houses. Walk the driveway. Use your key in the lock. Call out to your mother and hear her bustle in from the back garden where she has been hanging washing. Her sweatshirt sleeves are baggy with used tissues. Her open sandals reveal long toenails painted red.

'Let me look at you,' she says as she holds you by the shoulders and frowns. 'You've not been eating well.'

Hug your mother. Feel her softness and her new frailty but tell her that she looks good.

'Dad's just gone out for the messages,' she says as she leads you to the kitchen and starts taking condiments from the fridge. 'But he'll be back soon.'

Look out the window at the washing line your mother has abandoned: her flannel shirts, your father's colourless Y-fronts, their bed sheets filling with the wind like sails.

Clean your plate into the bin. Feel pudding on toast and four cups of milky tea drop like a stone into your stomach. Thank your mother. Go with her to the back garden and help her hang the rest of the washing. Ask while you work if there is anything else she needs doing while you're home. Tell her the garden looks nice.

'Ah, go on,' she mutters around the clothes peg held between her teeth. 'It's a state,' she shrugs, 'but I've never the time.' She nods towards the kitchen window and your father's silhouette, 'And no help.'

Sweep the leaves from the side lane. Drill holes for a hanging-basket hook. Dead-head the acanthus. Cut the grass.

'Don't belabour yourself on my account,' your mother says as she stands over you where you are weeding, holding a strimmer ready in her hand.

Tell her, 'It's no problem at all.'

'Well then, suit yourself.'

In the driveway next door, your neighbour Theresa is climbing out of her car. 'Ah, you're not putting him to work already, are you?' she says, her tongue curling over her upper lip as she winks at you in conspiracy.

Your mother measures a laugh. 'Might as well get some use out of him. Do you want some help there with your shopping, while the going's good?'

'Nah, you're all right,' Theresa says, 'I wouldn't do that to him on his birthday.' She hauls a bag of groceries from the boot and the new baby from the back seat. 'Do you want to have a look at him?' she asks and, without waiting for an answer, stands in her flower bed to dangle the baby over the wall. 'David,' she tells you.

Say, 'Hi, David.'

Take the baby in your arms. He is warm and smells of milk.

His eyes are clear as glass and his hands grope in the air for things you cannot see.

'Aw,' Theresa says, 'he's a natural, so he is.' She rearranges her shopping and takes back the baby, bracing his weight against her hip and steadying him with a muscled arm. 'Won't be long now till he's back with one of his own, and a little English accent on it.'

You can predict the expression on your mother's face: there is no need to look at her.

'A-babba, a-babba,' Theresa says as the baby starts to scream. 'I'll have to talk to yous later. No rest for the bleeding wicked.'

'Stop, sure I know,' says your mother, who has no other children. 'I worry about her,' she says, when Theresa has gone. 'And that worthless lout of a husband . . .'

She is still speaking but the buzz of the strimmer drowns her out. Apply yourself to your work: give the lawn a nice clean edge.

Take a shower, take a shit, shave, change your shirt. Check your watch and wonder how much longer you can leave off calling Henno and the lads. Find your father in the hallway tying his walking boots. Ask if you can come and watch him search for an answer as though the question is outrageous.

'Sure,' he decides. 'The company'd be nice. The company I suppose'd be a pleasant change.'

Follow your father out the door and down the street. Match your pace to his. Smile at the neighbours to whom he waves and wait whenever he stops to talk. Study your father: the purple flesh of his jowls, the grey in his beard, the hair in his ears. Listen to the ease of his conversation. Envy his comfort in the company of other men. Follow him through the lane.

Ask, 'So, how've you been keeping?'

'Sure, I'm walking, amn't I?'

Stop at the shop to buy cigarettes but tell your father you are planning to quit.

'How does it feel to be turning twenty-five?' he asks.

'Old.'

'It only gets worse.'

Follow your father to the coast, down the stone steps and out over the tidal plane where the sky soars heavenward and the town disappears. Feel the sand give beneath your feet and taste the salt on the wind. Stop into the Lifeboat where the barman is an old classmate of your father's. Answer his questions about London. Laugh at his jokes. Predict tomorrow's football scores.

'Birthdays is lucky,' the barman says. 'And I'll split the winnings with you.'

'See that you do,' your father says.

'I will. Sure, I said I will.'

'And I said see that you do.'

Thank your father as he stands you drinks. Tell him: 'I'll get the next one.'

'Get your hand out of your bleeding pocket,' he snarls, foam spraying from his lip.

Stay too long with your father in the pub. Watch daylight stretch itself thin above the harbour beyond the window. Field a phone call from your mother. Fill her in on your progress.

'If the doctors told him once –' she says.

'I know.'

'I won't wait on yous, so.'

Order whiskey after stout after stout after whiskey. Order toasted cheese sandwiches, peanuts and crisps. Feel the pub fill up around you, its heat and its conversation.

'Why is a woman like a tornado?' someone asks, and answers, ''Cause when she comes she screams blue murder and when she goes she takes the house.'

Go outside for a cigarette but tell your father you are trying to cut down. Listen to the regular clink of tacking against masts.

Sway.

Lean against the pub window ledge and look out over the harbour to the falling hills where a red sun dwindles to a flat line.

Shiver.

A girl is walking the beach, the wind in her hair and her jacket sailing. Watch her pick her way around puddles, over stones, up the slipway and out on to the road. Wallow in the sorrowful distance between you. Remember her with your every sense. Wave at her.

She is gone.

Take out your phone.

'Is it you?' Henno slurs when he answers. 'We were starting to think you'd forgotten about us.'

Tell him, 'Small hope.'

Find yourself in a smoking garden with Henno, Kellier and three nineteen-year-old girls.

'We're all going back to my gaff after,' Henno says. 'My Ma's away. We're having a session.'

'Your Ma?' one of the girls, a brunette, asks. 'How old are you, like, thirty?'

'I am not!' Henno laughs. 'I'm twenty-four years of age and not a day older. Ah no, it's just . . . Sure, she has no one else to look after her.' He leans over the girl's shoulder and flashes you a wolfish smile.

Kellier rolls his eyes and elbows you in the ribs. 'But would you not even do a half though, no? It's your birthday like, your *birthday*. Still and all I bet you get good pills in the clubs over there, yeah? What are they like? Mad, yeah? I bet they're mad.'

'So, Henno was saying you live in England?' the girl nearest you says. She has small features, wet eyes. She holds her glass with two hands and gazes up at you as though you might be in possession of some great secret.

Tell her, 'London.'

Kellier's eyebrows climb his forehead as he turns away. Henno mouths a filthy vowel of encouragement.

'I've always wanted to live there.'

'Well, why don't you go, then?'

Stagger down the harbour road, the world tilting in your bleary vision. Steady yourself against a telephone pole outside the sailing club and vomit on the wheel of a Land Rover. Feel your phone vibrate. Read Henno's name. Turn your phone off.

Let the sea wall lead you home through a wind that pulls at the corners of your eyes. Look out towards the islands, their flat shapes black against darkness. Watch the beacon of the lighthouse flicker on and off.

Make your way back through the lane, back along your silent street. Wrestle with your key in the lock and kick off your shoes in the kitchen. Creep up the stairs. Crawl into bed fully dressed. Listen through the wall to your father's troubled breathing as your ceiling starts to spin.

Fall asleep in the room where once you sheltered countless childish wishes. Sleep longer than you have in weeks. Sleep better than you have in months. Dream of long-forgotten futures that will come to haunt your waking hours.

Your mother is screaming.

Open your eyes.

The Navigator

When we dropped below the cloud, Dani's hand fell on my wrist. I leaned across her and looked out the window at a slab of iron sea, corrugated with waves and scratched with the small white V's of dissipating ship wakes.

'Did you know,' she said, 'that the Gaelic peoples descend from the Scythian Goídel Glas and an Egyptian Pharaoh's daughter?'

'Is that a fact?' I said.

'And did you know that an Irish monk, St Brendan, discovered America centuries before Columbus?'

'The Navigator,' I said. 'Yes. That one, I knew.'

The wing dipped. Squares of green land gleamed and vanished northward into haze. I felt my breath catch. Dani squeezed my thumb and smiled.

'Are you okay?' she said.

When Dani was born, I'd made noises to Elaine, with all the well-meaning arrogance available to the immigrant father, that we must do everything we could to provide our daughter with a transatlantic childhood: Fourth of July fireworks and the Paddy's Day parade, a month each summer at camp in the Adirondacks and two weeks in the Gaeltacht. But after Mam died, and I'd sold the house in Coolock, it was easy to put things off, to make excuses. Easy too to stay away from the Queensboro Irish Center, where a circle of blotchy-armed women, name of Colleen or Shannon or Erin, compared genealogies over mugs of milky tea. But one evening as we crossed the bridge on our way home from late study hall, Dani announced:

'I think, Daddy, I'd like to be a better Irishwoman.'

I let the 'woman' slide, though she was just shy of her fifteenth birthday, and downloaded *The Táin* to her iPad as soon as we got home. Before long, she was dragging me on school nights to uillean pipe recitals up in Yonkers and through the rain on Sunday mornings to Seán O'Casey matinees at the Irish Rep. Friday nights, while her classmates went in pairs to movies, she borrowed her mother's credentials and went alone to lectures on Roger Casement or Ernie O'Malley at Ireland House on Washington Square. And finally, one night as we waited for pizza, she brought out a binder stuffed with admissions information from Ireland's various universities, which she must have been assembling for months, and made her pitch.

'But I have tenure,' Elaine pleaded. 'I have full tuition

remission for you here.' Her lips were weak, her eyes very far away beneath their milk-bottle lenses.

'It's what I want,' Dani said, and she looked at me. 'Please, Daddy.'

While Elaine sulked, we hashed out a plan over double pepperoni and garlic knots. I'd cash in all the personal days I'd been hoarding for the past two years, have Georgette hold my case-load over for a week that summer, and Dani and I would jet off for my first trip back in fourteen years, her first trip ever, with a view to checking out some schools in Dublin and one in Galway, plus discover the heritage, plus spend some quality time together – just the two of us. My father had died when I was in my teens, and I hadn't heard from his side of the family in years. On my mother's side there were some cousins scattered through Cabra and Kimmage, but I could no longer picture their faces, never mind figure out how to get in touch with them, even if I'd wanted to.

We checked into a featureless hotel for nomadic men of business by the Grand Canal, in which Georgette and AmEx miles had secured for us a junior suite. There was a couch, a phone, an enormous TV, and two bedrooms separated by a locking door.

'The name Dublin,' Dani read from her iPad, 'appears in the record as early as the writings of Ptolemy the First, around 140 AD. It derives from the Irish Dubh Linn, meaning Black Pool, which is to say, the area of dark water where the Rivers

Poddle and Liffey meet. The city's been a Viking garrison, a Norman stronghold, and was briefly the second city of the British Empire.'

'Briefly,' I said as I reached into her closet for the suite's lone ironing board. I set it up at the foot of her bed and spread out a shirt.

Already, Dani had hung the outfits she'd spent the guts of the past week devising: a tweed blazer over a vintage T-shirt; a white blouse paired with ripped black jeans; a navy polo neck and a charcoal pencil skirt. Beneath each was arranged a pair of shoes: tan derbies, white Chuck Taylors, brown ballet pumps with a bow. And on the shelf above them were three dossiers culled from her binder, with many tongues of Post-its hanging from their edges.

The next morning, and for two mornings following, we toured libraries and lecture halls. Dani asked questions about borrowing limits and digital resources before heading off to meetings she'd scheduled with professors. Each time I stood for a moment to watch her walk away, her dossiers hugged to her chest, and each time I felt proud and vindicated for having raised a girl so capable. Never at her age would I have thought to arrange meetings like these, much less imagined how to go about it, or what to say if I had.

At university, it had felt as though my classmates and I belonged to separate worlds. They, it seemed, had been bred to feel comfortable eating in wood-panelled dining halls and drinking in cricket pavilions, whereas I had needed to work hard to fit in, and never did. I had earned the right exam points but not at the right secondary school, had honed the knack for argument but couldn't shake off my accent. From day one, I suspected – and when I graduated with honours but no offers, while they strolled towards the King's Inns with 2.2s, I knew – that I would never make it in the law in Ireland. I thought that America might be big enough to fit me in, applied to a dozen places and was rejected by all but one tiny school in Maryland. When I got there I found the same entitlement, the same unwelcome. And I found those things at the non-profit that gave me my first job, in the courtroom where I tried my first case, at the firm where I made my first million. Now Dani, I thought, had a chance to skip all that.

In the afternoons, while I read and wrote emails, she called Elaine and reported back to her about faculty ratios or alumni networks or internship opportunities. To me, she talked about the things that really mattered to her. Trinity, she said, was all city life and storied marble eminence (not to mention shoulderless boys with nicotine fingers and the poet's stare): she loved it. DCU and UCD were suburban, corporate, anonymous (also full of engineers and farmers; also much, much cheaper): she didn't love them.

But more importantly, to me anyway, she seemed really to love the city. We toured the Castle and the GPO, Christ Church and Kilmainham Gaol. I relived the mix of brief awe and enduring boredom that I once had felt on school trips, while Dani asked excited questions of the tour guide or, once, corrected him. After dinner, we people-watched from cafe tables and (Dani swore she wouldn't tell her mother) swigged Guinness in beer gardens, in alleyways or on rooftops. I felt the urge to list for my daughter the ways in which the place had changed – but I stopped myself. What, really, would have been the point? And how much, when it came down to it, could you really trust your memories of any time or place, especially your youth or, most especially, your home?

But some things Dani insisted on seeing for herself. And so, after picking up the rental car the night before we left for Galway, we headed out for a quick visit to the house where I grew up. The road was dark and lit in yellow pools. Traffic was sparse. The sky was starless, the moon a sliver.

'You know,' I said, 'this is only the second time I've driven in this country.'

'Did you know that settlement at Coolock dates back over three thousand five hundred years? A Bronze Age burial site has been excavated and dated to around 1500 BC.'

'Since you ask,' I said, 'I got my licence in the States so I could get your mother to the hospital in the event that you came early. I was twenty-eight, twenty-nine? Course, the first time, that is, my last time here, I was heading to the same –'

'What did she look like,' Dani said, 'your mother?'

'Your grandmother,' I reminded her. 'Do you not remember?'

'I was, like, a baby when she came to visit?'

'She looked . . . she modelled herself really, I think, after Maureen O'Hara. You've seen *Kangaroo*? Or *The Quiet Man*?'

'No.'

'My God. What do they teach you in that school?'

'Algebra, Macro-economics, Japanese, Romantic Poetry . . .'

'All right,' I said.

'. . . Enlightenment Dialectics, Daoist Philosophy, the Peloponnesian War –'

'She looked,' I said, as we turned on to the Malahide Road, 'glamorous. Or she tried to, anyway. Always had her hair set and her clothes well cut and spotless. She had this one coat, I remember, with these toggle buckles and a Nehru collar. She must've worn it nearly every day for twenty-five years. White! But she was careful with every little stain, stooped at the sink with her bleach and her rubber gloves at night, got it dry-cleaned every year at Easter. And she looked . . . I don't know what she looked like. She was a knock-out.'

I spun us on to the Tonlegee Road at the Cadbury's factory and we wound through the dark estates. Outside, fronting an unlit sports pitch, the old grey-speckled three-over-two still stood. Its windows had been double-glazed, its porch closed in, its driveway cobbled and occupied now by a black Ford registered during the previous year. I pointed to the window above the driveway.

'I slept in there,' I told Dani. 'And Mam and Dad,' I pointed to the window next to it, 'were there.'

I remembered the fall-apart wardrobes that the old man had built himself, the yeasty smell of the little kitchen downstairs. I remembered my last Christmas home, when my cousins had laughed at my wingtips and I'd told my mother I'd met someone. She was bent at the sink, her shoulders hunched for a painful moment, and when she turned her lip was bitten but thrust towards me in challenge. 'Just be careful,' she'd said and returned to scrubbing her coat.

And suddenly I felt an urge to go and knock on the door and ask if we could come in. I remembered the man to whom I'd sold the house those years before, recalled his jeans and his stubbled cheeks and his running shoes. I imagined his vague recollection of me, his suspicion of my return and the charm I would use to conquer it. I saw through his eyes the wholesome picture my daughter and I would present, and knew that he would be powerless to resist us. Already, I felt the eerie, dream-like state into which I would enter in the hallway, the thrill of recognizing things that hadn't changed and the poignancy of finding things that had. The whole experience, I imagined, would be satisfying in the same way that pressing on a bruise is satisfying. But more than that, I felt a sense of opportunity, a chance to create a strong memory in Dani's mind, something she would return to when she was in this country by herself, or alone in the world once I was gone. I told her my plan.

She watched me with patience, her eyes glazing, clearing. When I was done, she resettled her glasses on the bridge of her nose.

'No,' she said. 'I don't think that's a good idea.' She knitted her hands in her lap, her break-it-to-him-gently pose. 'Look, if you don't go in, then in your mind it could always be like it was. But if you do, it either will be or it won't be, and you'll know for certain – and isn't that so much worse?'

She breathed slowly and with some effort. I looked up at the house. Its windows were still. I started the engine and pointed us back towards the city.

That night, after the light clicked off from the cracks around Dani's door, I lay awake, my body clock suspended somewhere in the mid-Atlantic. The sheets were crisp, but the window seals were poor, the room airy and damp in a way that seemed thoroughly Irish. I checked my watch and calculated that, just then, Elaine would be finishing up and hurrying home from the 42nd Street Library, where she was spending the summer on an archivist's residency. In the Main Concourse of Grand Central, she would stop for a moment to look at the stars constellated in gold against the vaulted ceiling's blue, and she would think, I hoped, of her daughter and of me.

I reached for my phone and dialled her number, and as the

phone rang I thought of the one time she had truly enjoyed a visit to Ireland, a post-engagement whistle-stop jaunt around the Burren of which, judiciously, we hadn't informed my mother. For four gloriously, improbably sunny days, we had stamped our feet in sawdust shebeens to fiddle-and-drum combos, borne the slap of the Atlantic breeze at the lip of primordial cliffs and stood rooted to the rocky spot as two white horses raced inches from our elbows in love-chase. I had felt surer about things than I would be for a long time afterwards.

The phone rang five, six, seven times, and when Elaine answered I heard Miles Davis. But then lightly, distractedly:

'Have you made it to Galway yet?'

My wife pronounced the word, and deliberately so, I thought, *Gel-whay*, the first vowel flattened and the second syllable stretched, as though the language from which it grew were too frail to withstand her tongue.

'We're leaving in the morning,' I said. 'Where are you? I thought you'd be –'

'I told you this.' Elaine paused. I tried to imagine what room of our apartment she might be in, but the stereo gave no clue.

She sighed. 'I finished early. Calvin's taking me to dinner.'

Calvin Barnes was a professor of something who sat on an admissions committee with Elaine. I'd met him once at a cocktail party at some dean's apartment in Gramercy, and hated him on sight. He wore a grey corduroy three-piece with maroon felt brothel creepers, spoke in full paragraphs and, as soon as he got drunk (which was quickly), gazed deeply into my wife's eyes, unashamedly at her legs.

'Where's his wife?' I said. She was a big noise, apparently, in magazine publishing.

'Somewhere,' Elaine said. 'Tell Dani love.'

'Don't drink too much,' I said.

After I'd hung up, I thought about going out to walk the canal bank or the perimeter of the Green, as I had done sometimes in my student days. I fancied an adventure, or a drunken binge the like of which I never had permitted myself back then. But I didn't go. I stayed, watching the weak moonlight angle on to the nightstand and listening to the night dogs yelp, while in the other room, my daughter slept.

I woke the next morning feeling sluggish, as though I'd been stepped on. But once I groped my way to the shower and the peeling blast of good water pressure, I allowed my mind to range over the long westerly drive that lay ahead, and began to brighten. I made coffee in the room, listened to the radio as I dressed, and was raring to go, relishing already the thinness of sole of my driving shoes, as I knocked on Dani's door and waited for her emergence – but emerge she did not. I knocked again, heard a rustling. She opened the door a crack and held it on the chain.

'Morning!' I said. 'All set to –'

'Just give me fifteen.' My daughter's hair was madness, her eyes dark and fat.

'What happened to you?' I said and heard my voice find what Elaine called its Young Lady Range. 'Did you go out last –'

'Please,' Dani said. 'Fifteen.'

The door clicked shut. I wheeled my case to the lobby and, sitting beneath a plastic palm tree by the revolving door, scrolled through the Google docs Georgette had shared. An antitrust defence was in danger of falling apart a little less than a month before going to arbitration. I sent a stern but polite reminder to the client, some gentle reassurances to the partners, cc-ing Georgette on each and feeling negligent, detached.

When Dani finally materialized she looked transformed. She had gone with contacts for a change and her eyes seemed brighter than ever. Her skin was pale, her hair dark from the shower.

'Ready?' she said.

I followed her to the car and loaded our cases into the trunk.

'So,' I said as I programmed the GPS, 'where did you get to, then, on this wild night out of yours?'

'If you must know, I had three cocktails at the hotel bar. That's the whole story.'

'Did you talk to anyone?'

'No.'

'Did anyone talk to you?'

'Some dude in a suit tried to –'

'Jesus, Dani.'

'But I pretended I didn't speak English.'

I laughed: I couldn't help it. We crossed the Liffey at Kilmainham.

'Look,' I said, 'no harm done, I suppose. And probably best if we just say no more about it, yeah? But maybe, don't tell your mother? I wouldn't want her to worry. To be honest, I don't know which of us she'd be maddest –'

'That obelisk,' Dani pointed out the window at a marble monument looming over the Phoenix Park, 'commemorates the victories of Arthur Wellesley, first Duke of Wellington, in the Napoleonic Wars. Elsewhere in the park there's a monument to Pope John Paul II, who drew a quarter of the country's population to a special Mass in the year of his visit.'

'1979,' I said. 'I made my confirmation.'

On the far side of Maynooth, the cloud cover broke and rain pounded the car. Dani called her mother to describe the dreary territory through which we were passing. I pulled in at a Topaz somewhere before Athlone, took the phone and sent Dani out to fill the tank. The forecourt was empty save for a canary-yellow Volkswagen with tinted windows and outsize silver wheels. Its driver, a young guy, was filling up as well. He wore boot-cut jeans and an untucked stripy shirt. His hair was shaved close at the sides and gelled in a quiff on top.

Elaine was eating cereal and struggling with the cable box.

'How was Calvin?' I said.

'Oh, I don't think I'll be seeing him again for quite some time.'

Dani tapped on the window. I opened it and passed out my wallet. I watched her walk to the shop to pay, and the Volkswagen boy did too.

'What happened?'

Elaine groaned, embarrassed. 'You told me so.'

'He made a pass at you?'

'He's very depressed. And lost. And drunk too, of course. He really hates his wife. He touched my knee.'

'Jesus,' I said.

'And so I picked up his hand. And I gave it back to him. And I said: Calvin, hate her or don't hate her, you're going home to her right now.'

Dani stepped from the door of the shop as the Volkswagen boy stepped towards it. He said something to her, his hands in his pockets. She folded her arms and smiled.

'And did he?' I said.

'He passed out in the bathroom first,' Elaine said. 'But eventually, yes.'

The boy pointed towards his car. Dani laughed and pointed towards me.

'When are you coming home?' Elaine said, though well she knew.

The boy met my eye. Nothing passed between us.

'I love —' Elaine said, but then, 'Oh, the cable's back!'

I hung up. Dani walked the rest of the way to the car, her head bowed. She climbed in and I gunned the engine.

'What the hell was that?' I said.

She smiled. 'What was what?'

Galway appeared to us late afternoon in a mess of crowd-control barriers and bunting. Banners strung across the road cried the second-to-last day of a street theatre festival and signs in the windows of pubs summoned musicians for *seisiún*. Road-weary, we headed straight for the hotel, a self-styled 'inn' near the Spanish Arch that I'd allowed Dani to choose, with a heavy stone facade, faded carpets in the lobby and a stag's head and cutlasses and oil paintings on the walls. In the bar, a sweaty guy in a woollen jumper was playing an accordion.

'Isn't this great?' Dani said.

'It's something, all right,' I said.

Our room – a twin; the place was without suites – had exposed rafters, a floor that sagged in the middle, a TV bolted into a cabinet and greying doilies laid beneath the glasses on the bedside table. Through the window I could see the low roofs of the Claddagh hunched together, before them boats beached on sand and shale as their like had been for centuries, and beyond them the roiling darkness of the ocean stretching, stretching.

Dani seemed uninterested in exploring Galway, so I went out for dry burgers and oily onion rings and brought them back to the room. We ate watching a restaurant-transformation show as the holler and yelp of the bar downstairs rose to rattle our window. Dani studied her materials while I drank two scotches from the minibar. Later on, we changed into our pyjamas one by one in the bathroom and brushed our teeth side by side at the mirror. I turned off the light and lay in the dark listening to the crowds outside whittle down to a lone drunk singing a monotonous chorus. Eventually he sang himself out and the murmur of the river seemed to rise to fill the silence. Dani whispered:

'Dad, there isn't much of your stuff at home, is there?'

'What do you mean?' I said.

'Well, Mom has pictures and stuffed animals and stuff like that from when she was a kid. And that goofy *Chat Noir* poster from her dorm. And her guitar. I mean — mementoes. I mean your things. But you don't have any things, you know? I was thinking about this outside your mother's — my grandmother's — house. It's sad.'

I levered myself on to an elbow and squinted to see Dani's face. She was lying on her back staring at the ceiling, the horizon of her nose and chin aglow in the street light.

'Why, really,' I said, 'do you want to come to school here?'

'Did you know,' she said, 'that Brooke got into Harvard? With a full ride?'

Elaine's niece was a year older than Dani and a science whiz, who had spoken at nine and a half months but wet the bed until middle school.

'Yeah,' I said, 'I think I heard that.'

'And did you know that Stacey D'Albertino's older sister is on a Fulbright doing fresco restorations in Siena?'

'Did your mother tell you this?'

Dani shuffled on to her side and tucked her hands beneath a cheek. I wanted to tell her that she shouldn't compare herself to other people, to reassure her that she had all the time in the world – but three years was a long time to be away from home, and those years would lead to others that eventually would amount to a life. Dani would renounce parts of herself, and seldom notice when other parts changed. Who would she be, I wondered, when she was done here?

I tossed and turned all night on the hard mattress and gave up at first light. I showered quietly, dressed in the bathroom and went out, leaving Dani undisturbed. In the lanes off Abbeygate, soapsuds ran in gutters and people slept on kerbs. Men unloaded kegs or pallets of bread from the backs of trucks. I wound around by the quays and ordered coffee from a kiosk. The barista was a studenty type with auburn dreadlocks and a heavy gaberdine toggled against the morning chill.

'In town for the festival, is it?' she said.

'No,' I said. 'My daughter's looking at colleges.'

'I see,' she said as she passed me my cup. 'And what part of the States is it you're from? I've a brother over in Philadelphia. Are you anywhere near there?'

'Sometimes,' I said. 'We're not too far away.'

I brought my coffee to a bench by the waterside and sat to watch the boats. Tacking rang against masts in the wind and seagulls ran surveillance. I took out my phone and mapped the route to the university, mapped on a whim the distance back to Elaine. Then I followed the quays back to the hotel, where I shared an elevator with a trio of golfers in bucket hats and windbreakers. One read from a guidebook with a Midwestern twang. He dwelled on words like 'authentic' and phrases like 'time immemorial'. I wondered what my daughter's take on that vocabulary would be, what any of those words might mean if she heard or spoke them.

The room smelled of sleep, coffee and burned toast. I found Dani sitting cross-legged on her bed tapping her iPad and eating an apple.

'I was hungry,' she said and fixed the glasses on her nose. 'I didn't know where you were, but I got you some things anyway.'

On a cart by the TV, two trays held a baker's basket, a dish of preserves, a picked-over fruit salad and a plate with a plastic lid. I took the plate to the desk and uncovered a stack of fried meats and a halved tomato shining in a slick of fat.

'Do you know,' Dani said, 'how they make black pudding? It's really an interesting process. First —'

'If it's all the same to you,' I said, 'I'd rather remain in the dark. What are you writing there?'

'Thoughts.'

'Care to share them?'

'Nope.'

She pushed the iPad aside and laced her fingers between her toes. Her toenail polish had chipped. I cut and speared a sausage.

'Then let me ask you this,' I said. 'Just now, in the elevator —'

'Listen,' Dani said, 'about today. And don't be mad.'

'Mad?'

'I was thinking, maybe, of not going.' Her mouth opened, closed. 'It's just — I feel like I have all the information I need already, is all.'

I wiped my lips and pushed my plate away.

'But you haven't even —' I said. 'And after we've driven all this way?'

'I know.'

'Is there something you want to tell me?'

Outside, hoarsely, someone started up a verse. A guitar rasped into life a half a beat behind it.

'Oh, for God's sake,' Dani said. 'I've had it up to here with all these fucking sad songs.'

I crossed the room and sat on the edge of her bed. She stared into her lap, hair covering her glasses. I brought my ear down close to the mattress and looked up into her face. She laughed but her eyes were dull.

'Are you mad at me?' I said.

'Mad at you? Why would I be?'

My daughter drew her knees up to her chin and stared out the window. I followed her gaze over rooftops, past chimney-pots, along the pier and westward, out over the sea.

Date Due Receipt

05/04/2017

Items checked out to

Gill, Cora

TITLE Just one day / Gayle Forman.
BARCODE 30020002031815
DUE 25-05-17 00:00AM

TITLE An empty coast / Tony Park.
BARCODE 30020002177584
DUE 25-05-17 00:00AM

TITLE Over our heads / Andrew
BARCODE 30020002164525
DUE 25-05-17 00:00AM

Graduation

Martin Cleary, in suit and tie, carried two takeaway coffees across the square. The morning was fresh and bright – suitably collegiate, Martin thought. The water in the canal basin shimmered as it only ever did before noon.

Ronan rose from the bench by the door of Martin's apartment building and accepted with two hands the cup his father offered.

'Get that down you,' Martin said.

Ronan raised the cup to his lips. He was freshly showered but his hangover showed in red eyes half-screened by a curtain of lank hair. On his feet were a pair of motorbike boots he swore would not appear in the photographs. One of Martin's dark suits hung loosely from his shoulders.

'Good night, then?'

'I think so.'

'It was good to be able to put you up. Less so to be woken at three in the bleeding morning. Where were you?'

'Haven't a breeze.'

'You drink too much.'

'So do you.'

'Maybe,' Martin laughed. 'But I'm too old to change.'

They set off together down Pearse Street, Martin leading and Ronan looking around him at the collage of broken-down pubs and new sandwich shops that made this part of Dublin.

'Have you spoken to her yet this morning?'

'Texted. But I'll ring her when I leave you.'

'Did you tell her you'd missed your bus?'

'Yeah.'

'And what did she say about you staying?'

'What do you think?'

They entered the college through the wrought-iron gate on Westland Row. Ronan led the way past the stone steps and oak doors of the Physiology and Zoology buildings. In a green space bordered by apple blossoms, two bearded boys were throwing a frisbee. Nearby a cluster of students in dark gowns led their families to the deck of the cricket pavilion. The girls wore clicking heels. The boys slouched with their hands in their pockets. The parents linked arms.

'Do you have to pick up your gown and all?'

'Yeah.' Ronan drained his coffee cup and threw it, hit a metal bin with a clang from ten feet. 'But I have one reserved.'

On the tree-shaded benches by the cricket pitch, tourists in windcheaters huddled over maps. Martin and Ronan passed beneath the granite edifice and gothic windows of the Old

Library building and continued on into Front Square, where Martin savoured the sensation of well-tended grass, white-columned buildings and glinting cobblestones. He reached out and ruffled Ronan's hair, at once regretting it as his fingers caught.

'You need a haircut.'

'I know. I meant to get one but I ran out of time.'

'Do you have time now?'

'I suppose. Do you know somewhere close?'

The barbershop Martin used was in a basement room of gilt mirrors and soft leather couches. It smelled of scalp and shaving foam. There was only one other customer in the place.

'This one, Keith,' Martin told the barber as Ronan climbed into the chair.

Keith nodded and tied the cape around Ronan's shoulders. 'How do you want it, so?'

In the mirror Ronan's eyes met Martin's for a moment. 'Short,' he said. 'I suppose something clean and . . . something short.'

The electric shears buzzed as Keith went to work, dropping lengths of hair over Ronan's shoulders to the floor. The barber filled a water bottle and sprayed the top, then sliced in with a long-bladed scissors. When he was done, Martin felt as though he could make out more clearly some of his own features in the boy's reflection. Ronan had his father's chin, his father's nose, his father's eyebrows framing Anne's dark eyes.

'Cheers, Keith,' Martin said as he paid.

'See you again.'

They stepped out into the light. Grafton Street was getting busy. Ronan checked his phone and nodded in the direction of the college.

'Look, I'd better get going.'

'Exam hall, right?'

'You know where that is?'

'I'll find it.'

Ronan tilted his head and squinted up at his father. 'Look, will you sit with her?'

'I imagine so.'

'Good.' Ronan nodded.

'Here, do you need some money?'

'You're grand.'

'Just let me buy you a few scoops later.'

Martin took a hundred-euro note from his wallet. Ronan's eyes widened. He laughed.

'How much do you think I can drink?'

'Go on, I said. Just take it.'

Ronan eyed the money. 'Thanks. And for the couch. And the coffee.'

'Listen —'

Ronan tugged at his lapels. 'And the lend of the suit.'

'Of course, my pleasure but —'

'And the haircut.'

'Any time.'

'I suppose I'll look good in the photos for you now.'

Ronan made to go but Martin took his hand. In an hour they would be together again but they would not be alone. With the hair gone, Martin could see more clearly the angular set of Ronan's jaw, the hard lines of his cheekbones, the height of his forehead. He had small ears, a small mouth, lines already at the corners of those dark eyes. His Adam's apple, nicked from shaving, seemed enormous. The suit fitted him poorly but still he looked great. He was a man, entirely himself. Martin couldn't keep from blurting out:

'We don't look that alike, you know.'

Ronan frowned. 'I know.'

'No,' Martin said. 'I mean, I feel that sometimes we do . . . But a lot of the time . . . It's not there is what I mean. Sometimes I don't see it.'

'Yeah.' Ronan looked away over his shoulder.

'I used to think you looked more like your mother.'

'No, not really.'

'No, you're right, not really.'

A liveried doorman smiled as he admitted Martin to what Anne called the Temple of Mammon: a high-ceilinged lobby with marble floors and brass fixtures. Martin asked a girl promoting store credit cards where he could find the watches and followed her directions across the lobby and down the stairs. He paused at the near end of an L-shaped counter and bent to peer in at a selection of women's watches, studying their jewelled faces and imagining how the blue felt of the boxes might feel against his fingers. Without realizing, he had begun to slide back into the past as he had sworn that morning he would not. He stopped himself, moved away from the women's section and along the length of the counter to the far end, where the men's watches were housed. His preference was for a very simple gold piece with a notched face and a dark brown strap, but he knew it wasn't right. The right one was a chunky steel affair with a clever-looking double clasp and a square face with no marks at all for the numbers.

Emerging into Grafton Street, Martin spotted Brian Glennan struggling towards him through the afternoon crowd. Brian was a balding, gangly man who stood at a great height that made his approach visible over long distances.

'Martin!' Brian shouted, jumping and waving. He fought through a gap in the throng and stumbled to Martin's side. 'Jesus, that's mental.'

Brian wore his fighter pilot's leather jacket and a pair of sunglasses that Martin had heard him refer to as his 'fuck-me shades'.

'How are you doing, Brian? You're looking fit.'

'Ah.' Brian shook his head. 'Fit to drop is more like. Sure, you know yourself. Ours is not to wonder why.' He lit a cigarette.

'How's Trisha?' Martin said.

'Still chugging along, more's the pity. But she's talking to me again, small mercies.' Brian lowered his sunglasses on his long nose. 'So, what're you up to? Shopping? Anything good?'

Martin held up the carrier bag. 'Graduation present. It's Ronan's conferrals today.'

'Oh, yeah? Nice. Congratulations. I went to Audrey's one last week.'

'And how was it?'

'Ah, I don't know. It was a graduation. Everyone wore hats.'

They stepped out of the doorway and walked together for a moment before stopping at the entrance to a cigar shop on College Green.

'And how about herself?' Brian said. 'Are you nervous about . . . ?'

'Having to talk to her?'

'Right.'

'Ah, it's not about us, you know? It's his day, after all. I think it's the least we can do. I reckon we'll survive.'

The corners of Brian's mouth turned down and his lower lip protruded. 'Fair enough, so,' he said. 'That's a beautiful and mysterious woman. Who knows how these things'll turn out?'

'Sure.'

'Well . . . Right you are. I'll love you and leave you, then.'

'Take care, Brian.'

'I can but try.' Brian moved away, his head bobbing again in retreat above the crowd.

On the steps in front of the exam hall, Martin felt a tap on his shoulder and discovered that he had strayed into someone else's photograph. He stepped out of the way only to find himself blocking another shot – another patient, adult kid standing between mother and grandmother, and father frowning at him from behind the camera. Martin made his apologies and retreated out of frame. He straightened his tie, looked out across the crowded square and allowed his eyes to skip from group to group. In the distance a girl carrying a heavy book bag was giving directions to a tourist. Martin followed her pointing arm to the corner of the grey dormitories and then travelled their line into a sky impossibly blue.

He felt his heart quicken as he began to make them out. Anne was walking between Ronan and a tall blonde wearing glasses and boots, the shape of whose body was untraceable beneath her gown. Martin brushed his jacket shoulders and smoothed back his hair. When Ronan saw him he broke from his mother and the girl, ran over and bounded up the steps.

'All right?'

'Grand, yeah.' Martin struggled to smile. 'Feeling better?'

'Much.'

'I ran into Brian Glennan.'

'Oh yeah?'

'He sends his congrats.'

'Good stuff. Brian Glennan.' Ronan grinned. 'Is his wife fucking him again?'

'No.' Martin laughed. 'No, she is not.'

Ronan looked at the bag in Martin's hand. Now, while they were alone for a last moment, was the time to give him the watch. But Ronan turned away too quickly and reached for his mother's hand to help her up the steps. Anne took Martin in with one quick glance and looked away towards the front of the square and the archway at the main gate.

Ronan presented the blonde. 'Da,' he said. 'This is Eve. She's in my class.'

'Congratulations.'

'Thank you.' Eve's voice was soft. She had a silver ring in her lip and wore tortoiseshell glasses. She was good-looking, small featured and clear-skinned in a way that made Martin think of kindness. She spotted what Martin assumed to be her own parents and made her excuses.

'I'd like to say hi too,' Ronan said. He shot Martin and Anne a cautionary glance and left his parents alone.

Anne held herself straight, her hands gripping her bag straps. Her make-up was applied expertly and sparingly and she had little jewelled touches here and there: jade earrings, an enormous amber ring on what once had been her wedding finger.

'So, you made it in safe?' Martin said.

'Yes.'

'You look well.'

'And you too.'

'How've you been?'

'Oh, fine.'

'And work. How's work?'

Anne looked at him from the tops of her dark eyes. 'Work is work. It's grand.'

'I'm fine by the way.'

'You always are, aren't you?'

After Ronan came back they took some awkward photos on the steps and then filed into the exam hall, Ronan and Eve together with Eve's parents, Anne struggling to keep up and Martin lagging behind. The kids went off to sit with their classmates before the dais and Martin and Anne sat together in the first row of seats arranged around the periphery.

The hall smelled of age and paper, its high walls adorned with smoky oil paintings of Elizabeth I and Raleigh, and many others Martin could not make out. There were stained-glass windows near the roof and one large window at the back of the dais through which shafts of blue and pink light entered. Families chatted amongst themselves. Martin sat with the bag in his lap.

'So,' Anne said after a time. 'His hair's short.'

'Yeah,' Martin said. 'You like it?'

'It's not bad, actually.' Anne's jaw muscles were working. 'And you let him sleep on the couch, then?'

'Yeah. It was no trouble.'

She snorted. 'I wouldn't expect it to be. But the couch? On the night of his graduation?'

'It's a one-bed apartment. Where would you like me –'

'Well, I wouldn't know how big it is.'

Martin swallowed hard and said, 'Listen. Let's not do this.'

'What?'

'Let's –'

'Yes?'

'Nothing.'

'Fine. That's absolutely fine.'

After a while, a door opened at the top of the room and a procession of academics began. They crossed the dais with heads bowed, shuffling in long robes. The Dean of School took the podium. He was middle-aged, vaguely Scandinavian-looking, and wore a furred hood, a green sash and a pair of stylish, thick-framed glasses high on his nose. The watch would suit him, Martin thought.

Once the Dean had made his opening remarks, the department secretary began the long roll-call of names. Martin's eyes wandered around the hall before settling on the back of Eve's head.

He decided he would try again. He pointed over and whispered to Anne, making sure of an even tone, 'Are they –'

'What?'

He thought of a word. 'Involved.'

'Ronan and Eve?'

'Yes.'

'He hasn't said anything to you?'

'No.'

'Well, then, it's not really my place.'

When all the names had been called and all the diplomas distributed, the Dean took the podium again. There was some cheering and some applause. Ronan and Eve leaned towards one another.

Martin bent down to be heard. 'You did a great job on him.'

'I know I did.' Anne was looking straight ahead. Her eyes didn't move.

Eve's father was a tall, thin, gentleman-farmer type. He looked like he belonged to a golf club and could run four or five miles without losing breath. Ronan, Anne, Eve and Eve's mother positioned themselves for more photos: beneath the Campanile; in front of the Old Library; between the stone pillars of the dining hall.

'You must be Ronan's father.'

'Martin.'

'Ken.'

The kids had their degrees now, presented as cylinders bound with blue ribbon. Eve cradled hers carefully at her chest. Ronan held his by his side like a rolled-up newspaper.

'You look like you're remembering the drive home from the hospital,' Ken said.

'Something like that. Is it that obvious?'

'To some.' Ken offered a cigarette. Martin shook his head. 'I'll tell you, though, the first time? Scariest hour and a half of my life. And we only lived forty minutes away. I crawled home. I remember every bump, every inch of that road.' A match flared in front of Ken's face. He puffed a ribbon of smoke and shook the match out. 'This is your first?'

'Only.'

'I've had three go through myself already.' Ken took his wallet from an inside pocket and opened it to show a creased picture of four little girls. The eldest was about six or seven, the youngest no more than a few months.

'Four girls,' Martin said.

'Outnumbered,' Ken winked. 'But never outmatched.'

Eve's mother beckoned as the others moved away.

'So, Eve's the baby?' Martin said.

Ken smiled. 'That she is.'

'And how are they doing? The others, I mean.'

'Some good. Some not so.'

They rounded a corner and came into a smaller, quieter square where the women and children gathered around a bench.

'When you think about it, though,' Ken said, 'it's ridiculous to expect that every one of them will just naturally be better than we are.'

'Right.'

'But the thing is, at the same time, it's absolutely necessary.'

Eve's mother handed the camera to a passing student, explained its workings and then marshalled the group. The two kids sat together on the bench while the parents stood behind them. Martin took his place between Ken and Anne. The camera flashed.

At a restaurant on Dawson Street, Martin waited with Ronan and Anne for the table she had reserved. They sat in plush armchairs in the front-of-house bar drinking complimentary cocktails.

'So,' Martin asked Ronan. 'What's next?'

Ronan set his glass down on the table and clasped his hands together between his knees. Martin admired the watch he'd managed to give while Anne was saying goodbye to Eve's parents.

Ronan looked to his mother. She shrugged.

'Actually, I'm thinking of taking a year off. I'm thinking of travelling a bit. Maybe Korea.'

'Korea.' Martin listened to his pronunciation of the word. 'What's in Korea?'

'Lots of things,' Ronan said. 'I'm just thinking of trying it. For a while. You know, while I can.'

'I think it's a great idea,' Anne said and ran a finger around the lip of her glass.

Behind the bar, a flat-screen TV showed a to-camera report from the street in front of the Mansion House. Martin found himself staring through a window at the back of his own head. He turned in his seat to look but a hostess came to tell them their table was ready. He picked up his glass, and together the Clearys stood.

Stations

The following year, the twenty-sixth fell on a Sunday. Mangan woke late to the howl of a neighbour's dog. He breathed through his nose the coolness of the other pillow. His arm beneath his ear was numb; he waited for it.

At length, blood resumed its course and the fingers were his again. He rose and dressed, crept to the bathroom, lathered and razored his jaw. A crisp draught slapped his cheek as he knotted the tie at his throat. The suit was made of blue serge, its pockets wide and deep; he'd bought it only months before but now it sagged in the seat. Downstairs, he ate a slice of toast broken around a fried egg and drank a pot of black coffee at the sink until his hand steadied. Magnets held faded drawings to the fridge's face behind him. Heaps of papers cried old news from the worktop at his elbow. Around noon, he set out for the Lifeboat, the sky above him loaded. His neighbours' driveways mostly were empty, their curtains still.

At the far end of the laneway out of the estate, three boys not much older than Rory hunched in a glower of smoke. They were decked in gleaming trainers and drainpipe trousers, on their fingers rings too brightly gold to be made of gold. One of their phones whimpered tinny hip-hop. Mangan kept his eyes on the opposite wall's graffiti and caught his toe as he passed on the pavement's broken seam. The boys rocked together, honked together with laughter.

'There goes the man, now,' drawled the tallest of the three. Through his dark hair there shot a lightning bolt of bleach, and his sideburns were sharpened to points.

Outside the Lumsdens' house on the corner a postman dismounted his bike. Ivy licked a wall of the sagging porch. At the front door, a stooped figure dressed in green appeared.

'Is that young Mangan, there?' Brendan Lumsden said and squinted down his nose. 'Tell us now, will you ever be calling around the shop again to see us?'

Often as a child, Mangan had gone with his mother for sweets to the newsagent's Brendan and his wife ran together on the harbour road. Sunday after Mass had been his mother's time for presenting herself to the town, for doing messages and for paying visits and for stopping to swap scandal. Brendan now ran the shop alone, but still he referred to himself in the plural.

'To be honest,' Mangan said, 'I've been keeping myself to myself.'

'That's the good thing sometimes,' Brendan said. 'I suppose.' He sat on the garden wall to knead an ache from his thigh.

Beside him the panicles of a butterfly bush reached heavily towards the pavement. The postman handed him an envelope and wheeled away one-legged.

'It is,' Mangan said.

'But sometimes, though, it isn't, do you know that way?'

More recently, Sunday had been his day about town with Rory. Brendan's wife played peek-a-boo with the boy from behind the shelf of firelighters, called him 'the up-and-coming heartbreaker' and, once, daubed ice cream from his cheek with the collar of her cardigan. Her name was Peggy but Rory called her 'Veggie'. She and Mangan's mother had been in the hospice at the same time.

'Isn't it a hard old world?' Brendan said.

'It can be,' Mangan said.

He took his leave then, feeling at fault for not having inquired after Liz. But that might have meant talking about Annette, and he was glad that Brendan hadn't mentioned her. He crossed the street and wound towards town in the cool shade of the ice houses. Compressors hummed behind rusting doors with hinges glossed in rime, above which seagulls rode the gusts from sea to shore. One scaly-toed bird perched on the lip of a plastic crate where a soup of swim bladders ripened. It shuffled its feathers, goggled at Mangan, lowered its beak in stench.

The tremor came again to his hand as he rounded on to Strand Street, but at the Lifeboat he found only darkened windows. The pungency of old stout seeped from cracks in wood and grout. A handwritten sign affixed to the pub's door announced a family matter. Mangan sucked his teeth and hid the hand in a trouser pocket. He looked across the street towards the rise of St Patrick's bell tower, roofed in crumbling shingle and pointed with a cross. From the fine grain of the building's brick, some luminous mineral shone.

After the funeral, he had started going to Mass again. For months, Annette spent her weekends in bed and Rory's room remained untouched. But then, one Sunday morning, he read in the bulletin that the church was accepting donations. Soon afterwards, Annette saw a boy at the rugby pitch wearing a Lions jersey with a fraying sleeve. Mangan had come home to find her sitting at the kitchen table, the jersey spread beside her with its sleeve newly stitched. Within a week, Rory's things were boxed, his bed and bookcase sold. A week later, Annette was gone.

Mangan had not been inside the church since, but now he felt the pull of blue stained glass and columned portico. He crossed the street to find the font empty save for a brittle sponge. The nave, where two old women knelt, was dark and stale. Along one wall, the confessionals were curtained in fraying purple velvet, and between them, cast in plaster, were the Stations of the Cross.

Mangan walked the Stations, from judgement to crucifixion, the heels of his shoes creaking on the church's well-walked boards. He paused at the fourteenth where the Saviour's body, wrapped in linen, was laid to rest in the tomb as the women of Jerusalem wept. Next to the cast was a handmade banner that read *The Resurrection*, and below that were a number of children's drawings in crayon and coloured pencil: Jesus, chest emblazoned with a red S, soared above Metropolis; Jesus, beardless, ate cereal and toast at a kitchen table. Mangan touched the clots of crayon where the lines unsteadily crossed. He dropped a coin into the box by the grotto and lit a candle.

On the church steps, the afternoon broke across his face. Shoppers and gossips and idlers and kids criss-crossed the town's main thoroughfare. Cars jutted from parking spaces like broken teeth. Skateboarders kick-flipped around a mother dragging a child. Mangan quickened past the SuperValu's trolley bay and the deli's flowerless planters. A mossy lane led him to the beach where a salt wind rose to meet him. Tang of ozone filled his throat as he climbed the steps to the dunes. The tide was out and the plain was smattered with rocks and hunks of wrack. The headland curved around a bay whose restful water covered rip tides. The sea below the islands, and the sky above them, were steely. But between them, where the dark cloud lifted, a pale light shone.

Mangan took the half-bottle from his inside jacket pocket. A lifeguard watched him from a deckchair perched at the crest of a dune. He was young and he wore a yellow sweatshirt and he was waving. Mangan waved back. The lifeguard let his hand fall. He rose and stepped lithely as the sand at his flip-flops crumbled.

'Well?' Mangan said.

'This is a public beach.' The lifeguard's lips were thin and chapped and his nose was broad and pink.

'I know where I am.'

'So, you'll have to put that away, then, won't you?'

Mangan raised the mouth of the bottle to his lips. He wanted to drink it off in one but the liquid burned in his throat. He drew a cuff across his chin and bent at the hip and spun. The bottle sailed against the sky and disappeared into a snarl of sedge grass.

'Satisfied?' he said.

On the promenade, a woman pushing a stroller stopped to shake her head. Two little girls, straddling bikes that were far too big for them, pointed. Mangan heard on the wind in snatches the sounds of waves and of gulls. His bones felt out of joint, his heart like melted wax.

'I have real work to do,' the lifeguard mumbled. 'Please, just get out of here.' He turned his back and reascended swiftly to his watcher's chair. Mangan crept out of the lifeguard's sight and lay down in the shade of a dune. He dug his fingers into the sand until the skin pushed back at the nails. Then, for a long while, he felt nothing.

The sun dipped.

Between the islands and the shore, fresh whitecaps rose and

fell. Oystercatchers waddled in twos and threes and bent to beak at rock pools. The incoming tide ran from ridge to sandy ridge, seaweed giving form to its movement in streelish trails. Mangan felt a breath of wind against his cheek and opened his eyes. No one approached him from across the sand. The cloud lifted further from between the islands and the light shone brighter.

Are You Still There?

I first met Carol at a poetry reading in a bookstore off Lafay-
ette, up on the balcony level, where a pair of concrete pillars
framed the view of the lectern. It was a wet night; we got chatting as we stood to dry ourselves beneath a heat vent, the smells
of the subway rising from her coat. She had green eyes and a
laugh so loud and full I felt it in my chest. She worked, she said,
for an arts foundation that endowed one of the evening's
readers – a professor from the English Department where I
was working towards a doctorate, whom I wanted for my
supervisor and whom I cornered by the drinks table once the
reading concluded. The professor wore a blue silk scarf wound
carelessly around his throat. He agreed in principle to work
with me, and then I went looking again for Carol, but the only
remaining sign of her on the balcony was a small wet heel-print
darkening the scuffed boards. I stared at it, feeling certain that
an opportunity had passed me by.

So, when we chanced to meet again a few weeks later at a
party on the Upper West Side, I was determined not to let her

leave my sight. I followed her from room to crowded room, into and out of awkward conversations, and, in the early hours of the morning, on to the fire escape to smoke a joint and watch the water towers, the windows, the whole city quiver and stir and grope its way towards the light. Soon, I was spending most nights in her studio apartment above a taqueria in the East Village. We talked ourselves to sleep and woke up to make love, her warm breath at my ear shuddering to rise and fall. When she caught the flu, I spent a three-day weekend bringing her soup and tea. And when a cab knocked me off my bike, she ran through the snow to my hospital bedside and refused to leave at the end of visiting hours.

'You'll have to drag me out of here,' she said, eyes ferocious.

'Oh, I get it,' the nurse flung up her hands. 'Y'all in love.'

When Carol's landlord raised her rent, we decided to get a place together. I was frightened by how quickly things were moving, but excited finally to get away from graduate-student housing – an ex-project crammed with small apartments chopped into smaller ones, with door hinges stiff from countless coats of paint and hallways echoing with the lonely bleats of video games. Carol and I couldn't afford much, but after a few weeks we found a one-bed in Carroll Gardens that her salary and my stipend could just about cover. I'd got used to living in Manhattan, and the two-train subway ride seemed to take an age. But the apartment was clean, with high ceilings and two real rooms. And the neighbourhood was safe and grown-up

feeling: neat streets of four- and five-floor walk-ups with children's bikes chained to railings. We unboxed our clothes and
positioned our furniture, hung our pictures on the walls
and set up the cable. On weekends, we scoured flea markets
and came back with a suite of French lamps, a cut-price Moroc-
can rug with cigarette burns at the edges.

Before long, though, it became apparent that we had gotten
in over our heads. We could no longer conceal the habits and
tempers we'd managed until then to keep hidden from one
another, and it turned out that we'd been over-optimistic about
our finances. When a fellowship I'd been banking on failed to
materialize, Carol had to call her sister for a loan. The sister
was five years older, and married in New Jersey. She stared at
me hard over a plate of ribs in a barbecue place near Penn Station, dabbled her fingers in a bowl of lemon water and asked
Carol when she was planning to call their father. He, I'd gathered, was a dry drunk who had raised them both alone upstate
and never quite forgiven either of them for leaving. Carol nodded her head, sipped a glass of water and made a promise I
knew she had no intention of keeping. Right then, I wanted to
take her by the hand and run with her out of the restaurant and
keep running.

Over the next few months, Carol's job had her working
sixty-hour weeks, while the qualifying exams for which I was
preparing kept me in the library even longer. In the mornings,

we kissed each other quickly with crumbs of sleep on our faces, and at night we sprawled on the couch too burned out to do much of anything else. She seldom laughed. We made plans to spend Saturday afternoons in the park together, then got into roaring fights on Friday evenings and spent whole weekends avoiding one another. On those days, I brooded over how, in such a short space of time, I had come so completely to depend on Carol, and wondered what I would do if she ever decided to cut me out of her life.

At better moments, I fantasized aloud about taking a holiday, and Carol began to ask questions about the place where I'd grown up. I told her that we couldn't afford transatlantic flights, but in truth my reluctance came from someplace deeper. In three years, I'd been back to Dublin only for two Christmases, and each time I'd found the city a little more unfamiliar, as though upon landing I'd been jolted from a long and restless sleep. My friends had found new partners and routines or moved away altogether, and my mother was becoming ever more the wife of a man who was not my father. I could tell, though, that the idea of the trip had become important to Carol, and I wanted to try and show her that she was important to me.

After my exams, I coaxed a travel grant from the department, promising to spend a couple of days reading manuscripts in the National Library, and Carol put in a request at work for some vacation time. We packed and took the train to JFK and flew for the first time together, Carol jittery with nerves despite an Ambien. We landed at dawn, blearily caught a cab, sailed along the motorway. On the front step of what I still thought of as Eamonn's house, Carol gripped my hand as a shadow moved behind frosted glass.

My mother answered the door and stood for a moment to look at us. She had cut her hair into a prim old-lady style, had given up squinting and pretending and had bought glasses. She told me I looked thin, told Carol she looked *exotic*. In the living room, we sat to watch the morning news with Eamonn, who peered at the TV along the full length of his nose as though he were above these events but monitoring them nevertheless. When my mother entered with a clattering tray of tea, he leaped to his feet to take it from her and set it down on the coffee table. He brought her a cushion, her slippers.

'There you are now, missus,' he said.

My mother rolled her eyes. 'He's a fusser.'

Once Carol and I had unpacked, we took a trip to Marlay Park, and I tried to remain calm as I watched the hitherto separate parts of my life collide. Eamonn and I drifted ahead through the topiaried grounds and the walled garden, chatting without saying much of anything. Every now and then, I'd glance behind at my mother in faded tracksuit bottoms and mud-caked walking boots, Carol in bright leggings and white sneakers she was happy to ruin on the trails.

'Your mother's very nice,' she said that night as we lay together in the guest room.

I stared at the mottled ceiling, smells of strange detergent rising from thin sheets. I reached my arm around Carol's waist; she rolled towards me.

The following day, we went to help my mother in her allotment. Carol weeded around carrots while I raked and turned the soil and Eamonn lashed new creepers to the trellis on the dividing wall. My mother hovered between us, standing at our shoulders, pointing at our work and making vague but firm suggestions. After we had returned home and showered, Eamonn went to watch a match in the pub and Carol and I went with my mother to an Italian place by the Dodder. We ordered salads and pizzas and a bottle of wine as though we had something to celebrate. I tried to pay, but my mother insisted. We walked back to the house together, my thighs and back aching from the day's labour. At the foot of the stairs, my mother said goodnight and hugged me far too tightly, her fingers strong on my shoulder blades as though they sought to burrow there.

I was glad to spend the next two mornings and afternoons in the quiet of the National Library. I found a few small things of interest and beefed them up in my notes to keep the department happy. The first day, Carol hung around the house but kept me updated via Gchat on how my mother insisted they bake together, then drink tea and talk for two hours about the weather in New York. The second day, she went sightseeing, and in the evening I suggested a drink at a pub in Smithfield that had been my local as an undergraduate. We took the scenic route along Dame Street, past the Castle and Christ Church, Carol half-listening as I recited history I only half-remembered. We crossed the Liffey at a point too far to the west and got lost in a labyrinth of grey- and red-brick houses. It was quiet. Our steps echoed.

'It'd be nice,' I said, 'to live here some day, wouldn't it?'

Carol looked up at me, frowning. I smiled and kissed her forehead. We came to a junction and stopped a moment to get our bearings. I looked left and right, then chose what seemed the best direction.

'You know,' Carol said, 'I wouldn't want to move.'

'No,' I said, scanning the street for a landmark. 'I meant if we ever did. If we ever – you know. Some day.'

The light at last was failing. Carol crossed her arms and rubbed her hands along her elbows. Behind her was a blank wall discoloured from old rain. We cut down an alley lined with shabby flats, depots and yards with broken signs and rusted gates.

'I feel like you're not listening to what I'm saying,' Carol said. 'What I'm saying is you can't have *some day*. You have to make decisions.'

We found the square and walked the cobbled way beneath gas lamps and the distillery's chimney. Above us, two small red balloons were hurrying towards the Liffey. I watched them hold together, sliding against the dusk, and felt it within my power to reassure Carol – or to deny her.

The pub was just as I remembered it. Its taps ran with flat Australian beer and its rooms were packed and sweltering. Carol and I fell into a rash discussion about the way things were and the way things ought to be. Neither of us, it was clear, had a point or a position – just a gnawing sense of unhappiness, of dwindled expectation, which, as I spoke, I realized I'd felt for quite some time, and which, as Carol spoke, I felt begin to deepen. We left our second drinks unfinished and set off again for a taxi. I walked as fast as I could manage, Carol struggling to keep up.

The driver didn't know the way. I sat in the middle of the back seat and leaned forward to direct him through the wreckage of a Saturday night and out through the suburbs. We made the M50, went too far and circled back, criss-crossed roads that meant nothing to me and in the end found the estate by chance. Carol stood in the street as I paid the driver, blank windows staring down at her. She looked very small and very strong, and far away from me. In our room, she took her clothes from the dresser wordlessly and packed her suitcase. When she had finished, she plopped down heavily on the edge of the bed.

'This trip,' she said, 'was a mistake.'

I said nothing. I went to the bathroom, brushed my teeth with a trembling hand and stopped for a moment on the way back to listen at my mother and Eamonn's door. I realized that

I wanted them to hear us. The door was open a crack but I couldn't see their shapes. Eamonn snored like an engine. Back in our room, I found Carol under the covers. I climbed in beside her. She knifed away and pulled the duvet with her. The draught from the window was cold on my skin. I fell asleep and woke sometime later to the sound of Carol crying, her shoulder heaving against mine.

In the morning, we kissed my mother and shook Eamonn by the hand, thanked them both for having us and promised to visit again soon. In the driveway, Carol's face was pale, my mother's was knowing. I loaded our cases into the boot of the taxi and looked back towards the house as we rounded the corner, fully expecting to find my mother and Eamonn standing on the step to see us on our way, my mother chewing her nails in worry, Eamonn's heavy arm slung across her shoulder – but the door was shut.

As we rode in silence to the airport, I willed myself to make some gesture, to do something – anything – that might be the size of love. I kept willing myself as we divided for immigration, as we reconvened to wait at the gate, as we boarded and took our seats. After take-off, Carol passed out, her head against the window. Even in sleep her forehead was creased, her eyes not merely closed but clenched.

Back in Brooklyn, we circled each other for a few days until Carol had worked up her nerve.

'I need some time to think,' she said and called her sister to ask if she could stay with her. She stood in the hallway with a couple of bags at her feet and looked to me for a word – for punctuation, even.

And then she was gone.

I took her winter coat from the hall closet and held its lining to my nose. In the bedroom, I hugged her pillow to my chest and opened her dresser drawers. I ran my hand over the soft cotton of T-shirts and the rough nylon of gym shorts. I picked up all the little things she'd arranged on the dresser top – a framed photo of the two of us and one of herself and her sister, a perfume bottle, a porcelain saucer full of spare buttons and safety pins and lapel badges and earplugs – and put them down.

I went out drinking. At first, I haunted our old hangouts: the craft beer place where we'd spent Sundays over crosswords, the bocce place where Carol had thrown me a birthday party. But soon enough, I began to feel as though all the hipsters in those establishments were watching me – so I settled on six-packs and cigarettes in bed. I called her sometimes, knowing full well that she wouldn't answer, just to hear the easy bounce of her voice on the answer message. After a few such calls her sister called me back. Her husband, she said, was a prosecutor. 'And he knows where you live, motherfucker. He has a lot of friends on the force. So stop calling my sister or they'll never find your body.'

I told Darren and Emma about the sister's threat at the

department's welcome-back picnic. They were the first real friends I'd managed to make in New York. Their eighteen-month-old daughter, Sky, sat mewling in her stroller, her eyes blue and meaningless. We sweltered under a late August sun. Emma wore open-toed sandals and no bra.

'What an asshole,' Darren said, stuffing his moony face with a turkey sandwich. He was two years my senior in the programme but one behind in terms of progress towards a degree.

Emma laid her hand on my elbow. Darren watched her do it.

'You must be heartbroken,' she said. 'Really, you poor, poor thing.'

'Asshole,' Sky said, the word a bubble on her little lips.

'That's a grown-up word, honey,' Emma said and grinned at Darren as she punched his shoulder.

When I got home, I went looking for Carol's coat but I couldn't find it anywhere. I searched for her pillow but couldn't find that either. It was then that I noticed the big Rothko print missing from above the bed. The dresser top was bare. I checked the bedroom closet, the kitchen and bathroom cabinets: Carol's sweaters and cardigans, her Crock-Pot and her Cuisinart, her soft towels and her acne medication and her hair dryer – all were gone.

'She's moved out,' I told Darren that Friday at the Tiger's Tail, a sweaty, dollar-a-PBR joint on Amsterdam where our dissertation workshop met. 'She just let herself in when she knew I'd be out and took all her stuff away.'

'Jesus,' he said, 'that's *cold*.' He eyed one of the new MAs, a girl in brown-and-white wingtips, a cape and Warby Parkers. 'So, what are you going to do for rent?'

I rubbed my hands over my cheeks, hard enough to hurt. 'I hadn't even thought of that.'

My father, in his will, had left me a small inheritance about which I'd never told Carol, and which I'd always thought of as my exit fund: enough money to buy a ticket home and to sustain me through a few months of looking for work. It would be enough, I imagined, to square me with the landlord until the end of the academic year – but only just.

'Listen,' Darren said, 'me and you, next weekend. Let's get out just the two of us and watch a game, okay? I've cleared it with ground control.'

But in the end, he couldn't make it: Sky had a cold. I sat in the living room in my Yankees hat, an empty Sunday stretching out before me. I checked Carol's Facebook page – she hadn't posted since Dublin. I wondered where she was, what she was doing, if she missed me. The couch, bare of Peruvian throw or embroidered cushion, no longer felt comfortable but merely worn. The white wall beneath the empty pot rack was hatched with dark streaks grazed by saucepan lips. The corkboard above the desk – but hadn't the cards and the concert tickets and the love notes scribbled on Post-its all been there the morning before? Hadn't the Chinese tea set still been sitting on the window ledge, the glass candlesticks still centred on the kitchen table? I smiled – she had been back again, and might be back once more for the microwave and the TV and every other little thing of hers she missed.

I started to mix up my hours, to work from home whenever I could and to leave campus straight after class, but Carol never showed. At length I discovered that, as long as I was reading or teaching, I could go sometimes for a full hour without thinking of her. Slowly, I put a shape on the dissertation chapter I'd been drafting since the summer, got to know my students and felt some vague enthusiasm. So it came as a shock when Darren and Emma invited me over to their place in Morningside and broke the news of what they'd learned.

'Who's *Tyler*?' I said.

'Listen.' Emma showed me the lines of her palms. 'All I know is what I saw and what little she told me.'

'And why was she telling you anything?'

'I told you,' Emma said, 'we just ran into each other in the street. I had Sky with me. They were coming out of some breakfast place.'

'Jesus,' I said. '*Breakfast?* How long has this been going on?'

'Really, I don't know. It was only for a moment. I saw them before she saw me. She was embarrassed, I think. But Sky had dropped her little baby Kermit, and he – the guy –'

'Tyler,' I said.

'He picked it up and I don't think she would have introduced me or anything otherwise but –'

'So you don't really know anything, then,' I said.

The baby monitor screeched. Emma leaped to her feet.

I pictured this Tyler: tall and blond, with broken-in expensive shoes and a neck full of well-groomed stubble. I saw him peering back at me everywhere from the crowds on the platforms at Times Square and started leaving earlier in the mornings to beat the rush-hour hustle. I'd arrive at the library around quarter to seven, chain-smoke on the steps until it opened and then hurry through the silent stacks towards my carrel. And there I'd stay, with the exception of class hours or trips to the vending machine, until ten or eleven at night. I sped through my second chapter at a rate of fifteen hundred words per day, lost ten pounds and grew a patchy beard and chewed all my nails to the quick. I stood before my class on a rain-lashed Monday morning, more caffeine in my veins than blood. I opened my mouth to speak but realized that I had nothing to tell them. Twenty pairs of eyes pinned me to the wall. I sat back down, assigned some busy work and dismissed them early.

My supervisor summoned me to his office on a sunless corner of the fourth floor. The lone window was set in a wall of too-often-repainted cinder block. Most of the bookshelves were overstuffed, chaotic. But the eye-level one held an orderly line of titles whose spines all bore the professor's name.

'Okay, look,' he said, his suit sleeves shiny, 'I understand that you're going through some personal stuff right now. But let me just level with you brutally here – may I be brutal?'

'Please,' I said.

He tented his slender fingers. 'No one has time for any of that, okay?'

'Okay,' I said.

'Which is not to say that we're inhuman. We are in the Humanities, after all! Just – hey – don't bring it into work with you, okay?'

'Okay.'

'Okay?' he said as I watched, behind him, the clouds begin to break apart in a sudden, clattering rainstorm.

'Okay,' I said.

The rain continued for a full week. It battered the windows in roaring torrents and ran like a river in the streets. I woke at night with a racking cough that left me torn and sour, and decided that the smoking really would have to stop. So, once the storm moved on, I slapped a nicotine patch to my shoulder and bought a new pair of lightweight sneakers. I was still young, I told myself; there still was time for me. At dawn, I wheezed along the promenade by the river, where Carol and I once had strolled on summer evenings. I added a hat and gloves and thermals as the days began to chill, and when the paths became clogged with soggy leaves I switched to a treadmill at the gym.

The Monday after Halloween, I cleared my third chapter. And that Thursday I presented a paper based on it to a conference at NYU. Aside from my fellow-panellists, three people forwent lunch to sit in the over-lit and under-heated conference room. Two of them looked unsure as to how they'd gotten there, but one turned out to be a minor star in my field. He took me out afterwards for coffee, and suggested that I send him something for a collection of essays he was editing. I hadn't been able to publish anything since a handful of reviews during the first year of my MA in Dublin, so I caught a train uptown to my carrel and stayed there until I'd edited the chapter down to a submittable draft.

At one a.m., I splurged on a cab to take me home. And for the first time in a long time, I felt grateful to be in New York: to be lurching between the lights in the crush and blare of Midtown, then speeding across the bridge suspended high above the East River. The cab rolled past the no-name clothing stores of Downtown Brooklyn and hung a right at the rust-coloured arena that always reminded me of the carcass of a ship I had once seen marooned on rocks off Inisheer. We slowed on President, coasting between the lights. I paid the cabbie and climbed the stoop. Someone, two weeks before, had strung the railings with cotton cobwebs, and they remained, as did a gang of pumpkins on the lower window ledges, their features now soft with decay.

In the hallway, I smelled chicken stock wafting from an

apartment whose tenants I had never seen. I climbed the stairs and turned my key. The lamp by the window was lit. A coat I recognized was strewn across the couch, a pair of shoes set neatly on the floor beside the coffee table. Once, on a beach in Clare, a wave had knocked me off my feet, dragged me across the ocean floor and pushed me back and rolled me; I had tried to breathe but there was nothing but water. That's how I felt when Carol stepped from the kitchen.

'I still have my key,' she said unnecessarily, her smile an exhibit for a case already won. 'I've been waiting for you.'

'Hi,' I said, very aware suddenly of a lightness at my finger-tips. 'You've come for more of your stuff?'

She stepped towards me, the fullness of her lower lip squeezed between her teeth.

'No,' she said. 'I'm pregnant. I think it happened in Dublin.'

Her dark hair was shinier than I remembered it, her skin clearer. And when she bent to sit, she cupped her belly with a hand as though the gesture were the most natural thing in the world. We talked about what we'd both been doing for the past few months. I told her that I'd missed her, and she said she'd missed me too. Eventually we moved on to Tyler, who she said was just a colleague, then a friend, then a mistake. When she started to nod off, I insisted that she take the bed, and fetched the spare blanket and pillow from the hall closet to make up the couch.

In the morning, with nothing resolved, we walked to the

subway together and went our separate ways. I taught my class with a new and terrified energy, and I realized suddenly how young they all were, in their baseball caps and sneakers, their heavy coats that mothers had picked out. As I packed my bag, I wished them well for the weekend. They filed out with nods or a mumbled word, but Elizabeth Jordan lingered. She was a Psych major who always sat in the corner, rarely participated in group discussion and never spoke to anyone before or after class. But she wrote uncommonly well, with empathy and poise. She smiled at me, all teeth.

'Have a good day,' she said. 'I'm glad to see you're feeling better.'

I had half-forgotten her voice, New England-y and clipped.

'Excuse me?' I said.

She looked towards the door. 'No, it's just . . . I was thinking that you used to look so unhappy, is all. But now you look happy. You're happy?'

I thought about it.

'Yes,' I said.

She smiled again, that dour face flashing with bright dentition. And her eyes, so often careworn, seemed relieved.

The following night, Carol came over for dinner. While I prepared the food, we stood across from each other at the breakfast bar, my knife dipping into the flesh of vegetables, her hand darting to the bowl to snatch a slice of pepper or a disc of carrot.

'It's strange,' I said as we ate, 'the way things turn out. Isn't it?'

Carol set down her cutlery and wiped her lips. 'What do you mean?'

I shrugged. 'We were always so careful, is all.'

'Well, nothing's a hundred percent.'

'And we never even talked about –'

'We talked about it.'

'Yeah,' I said, 'for scares. But I used to think it would be the worst thing in the world, you know? We were so unprepared. Or I was. And all that stuff. But now . . . I'm just, I'm really glad you're back.'

She cut and speared an asparagus stem. 'I'm not really back yet, you know,' she said. 'But, do you want me to come back? And do *you* want to be here?'

I reached for her hand; she let me take it. And after dinner, without a word, she led me to the bedroom. We got under the covers together and lay there fully clothed. The sheets were soft and cool. Her breathing was high and quick. I woke in the night facing her. I'd always loved the way she slept, with her hands joined together beneath her head as if in prayer. I reached down to touch her stomach, expecting hardness, fullness, but she felt just as I remembered. She groaned and rolled over and I snatched my hand away, the feel of her in my fingers. On Sunday morning, after breakfast, she went to her sister's place to collect her stuff. And every evening that week we unboxed the things she'd taken and returned them to where they belonged.

For Thanksgiving, we gussied ourselves up and brought a

store-bought pumpkin pie to Darren and Emma's place. Carol sprawled out on the living-room floor and played self-consciously with Sky's stuffed toys and blocks. I joined Darren in the kitchen to help with the turkey and the stuffing, the cranberry sauce and the Brussels sprouts and the three different kinds of potatoes. He wore a T-shirt printed with an image of an armed Indian tribe and the legend *Homeland Security*, kept a bottle of gin on the draining board from which he took frequent nips. A green felt card table groaned under the weight of food. We chatted like in the old days but didn't know what to toast. Later, when Carol passed out on the couch, and Emma pleaded with a sugar-rushing Sky to sleep, Darren and I crept downstairs to the stoop with the last of the gin. The street was quiet, the avenue dark, but every window on the block was lit.

'This situation right here is really quite a situation,' he said and passed the bottle. 'You won't believe what's ahead of you.'

I took a swig and winced, passed the bottle back.

'Tell me about it,' I said.

And he did: the hysteria of night feeds and the calm of total sleep; the torture of teething and the joy of watching her grow.

'It's fucking agony and it's fucking magical,' he said. 'Is that good for you to hear?'

I wasn't sure.

Once classes broke, I called my mother. Eamonn answered.

'She's had a little spill,' he said.

He told me about the 'cold snap' that had recently hit Dublin. The Council hadn't enough grit for the roads and was importing it from the Continent. There was snow on O'Connell Street, a drift three inches thick against the walls of the GPO where Eamonn and my mother had gone together to mail their Christmas cards. On the way out, she had slipped on a patch of ice and fallen from his grasp.

'I had her,' he said, 'and then I didn't.'

She was in the Mater, with a pin in her ankle and a bedside locker stacked with get-well cards. Did I have any news I wanted him to pass along?

'No,' I said.

I hung up and called my mother's mobile. She answered on my fourth attempt.

'Hello, love,' she said, her voice groggy.

'I just spoke to Eamonn,' I said. 'Why didn't you tell me?'

'Ah,' she said, 'we didn't want to worry you.'

She launched then into a long description of her ward: the nurses who looked too young even to be out of school; the ten-strong Polish family who visited their mother en masse and stayed all day; the old man across the aisle who, she said, 'has good days and bad. No one ever visits, so I sit with him whenever I can.'

'Do the doctors let you out of bed?'

'They worry too much, those boys.'

'Listen, Mam,' I said, 'I have something I need to tell you.'

I did. And as she screamed, I couldn't help but smile.

'I wish your father were here,' she said through tears. 'He would have been so happy, so proud.'

'So do I,' I said.

I started, again, to worry about money, about what I'd do after graduation and how I'd provide for what I'd started to think of as *my family*. I told my mother that we'd be staying in New York for Christmas, and although she sounded disappointed, she said she understood. I quit buying coffee in the mornings, cancelled my journal subscriptions, took extra shifts tutoring at the Writing Center and sold all my big anthologies to the student union bookstore. When Carol came home and saw the shelves empty she looked as though she might cry, looked too as though she wanted to say something. But instead she removed my glasses and kissed my eyelids.

In the New Year, I compiled dossiers of syllabus samples and student evaluations to bring to the Modern Language Association's hiring fair. I'd managed to schedule three interviews, while Darren had arranged just one for the sake of testing the waters. We took the Amtrak to DC together and shared a room at the department's expense. In the mornings, we dressed in thermals and parkas and trudged through the snow to see panels. In the afternoons, I changed into a sports coat and took my number in the huge and echoing interview hall at the Four Points Sheraton.

At my first two sessions, I distilled my research and plotted my timeline for finishing. The interviewers nodded with feigned or tepid interest. But at my third session, I heard myself say that my 'wife' was expecting our first child. Professor Dessa Greene — a young, goofy Victorianist from a medium-sized university in western Indiana — brightened and produced on her phone an image of her own son, nineteen weeks old and frog-faced, who at that moment was touring the Lincoln Memorial papoosed at his father's chest.

'The thing I like most about our department,' Dessa said, 'is that they understand the need to balance your work with your life. We're a young faculty, and there'll be a place for your family with us if we hire you.'

I left feeling cautious but hopeful. I called Carol but she didn't answer. I caught the bus to Georgetown to meet Darren for burgers and beers. His own interview, he told me, had been a disaster.

'Fucking philistines,' he said. 'Wouldn't recognize subtlety of thought if it bit them in the face. This game is rigged, friend-o. We should've just got real jobs.'

At the next table, a group of business-school types in blazers and khakis sipped from heavy glasses of Ketel One.

'Look at these assholes,' Darren said. 'They're the guys who beat the shit out of me in school. So I beat them *at* school. And I stayed in school forever. And now school is almost over, and it's back to their rules again.'

I told him about Dessa Greene.

'The family man,' he snorted. 'Christ. The kid's not even born yet and already you're leveraging the poor little bastard. Well, good for you. That's how the game is played. Apparently.'

Carol wouldn't be persuaded to take things easy. She'd work, she said, for as long as she could bear it to stockpile personal days and extend her maternity leave. I rehearsed what I would say to her should the offer ever come from Indiana, tried to think of anything that might make her want to move.

We enrolled in a birthing class that met three evenings a week in a basement in Cobble Hill. The facilitator, Sarabeth – we were instructed never to use the word 'teacher', because 'this kind of learning comes from within' – padded barefoot from couple to cross-legged couple, whispering encouragements in a voice well suited to her work but even better to night-time radio. Carol breathed in sync with my count, which often was distracted and arrhythmic. 'You've been a student your whole goddamn life,' she said as I tugged her to her feet and fetched her shoes. 'Why is it so hard for you to learn this one easy thing?'

We rented a Zipcar and drove it to a mall in Jersey, Carol gripping the wheel around her belly because I'd never gotten a licence. The mall smelled clean and sweet, like new stationery. We bought a crib and a stars-and-moons mobile to hang above it, a changing table and something called a diaper genie. The disposable or plastic items were bulky and preassembled. The wooden things were packed flat in cardboard boxes. I carried them all to the car and from the car up the stairs to the apartment. We filled what little space there was in the big hall closet and in the drawers beneath the bed.

I packed a box with my binders and took it to my carrel. I felt as though I'd fallen behind. Whenever I wasn't working, I noticed a chill beneath my arms and in my throat. But then, one morning in late January – with three missed calls from Carol, a whole suite of furniture left to assemble, and a leafless tree branch bobbing to the beat of frozen rain outside my window – I realized that I was finished. I drank a flask of coffee and spent a night cleaning up citations. And the following morning, in a haze, I printed a manuscript copy of the dissertation and left it in my supervisor's mailbox.

With nothing to work on, I spent long hours alone in the apartment. Letters and baby books began arriving with a Dublin postmark. I spoke more frequently with my mother, who was off her crutches and keen to plan her first visit to New York. I checked the job boards hourly for updates, bought a lock for the toilet seat and covers for the electric sockets. I hit the gym both mornings and evenings, got my mile time down to seven minutes.

For Valentine's Day, I reserved a table at Carol's favourite place in Gramercy. But on the night, she said she felt too tired to go out. We ordered a take-out feast from the Japanese place on Court and gorged ourselves on edamame and gyoza and teriyaki. Afterwards, we lay on the couch flicking between romantic comedies. The baby was kicking. Of course, I'd felt it before, had marvelled over it with Carol in the night. But now it was just a nuisance. She dug her shoulder under my ribs. I groaned and reached out to help her.

'Not *now*,' she said. 'Jesus, just give me a minute? Just let me . . .' She pulled a pillow out from beneath her and sighed. 'That's better.'

The film we had settled on took place in London. The snow was too flaky. Everyone wore turtlenecks.

'You know,' I said, 'you're always pulling away from me.'

'What I am,' Carol said through her teeth, 'is seven and a half months pregnant. Have a bit of compassion, will you? I feel like a fucking boat.'

The film cut to time-lapse footage of Piccadilly Circus: the sun a fixed point on an endlessly spinning wheel; taxis scurrying through the streets like ants; our protagonist fixed at the centre of it all, unmoving. I realized that Carol was crying.

'Shit,' I said. 'I'm sorry.'

She shook her head but the sobs kept coming, catching in her throat with a strangling sound and stopping her from breathing. I ran to the sink to fetch a glass of water and held it to her lips. She tried to sip but gagged and knocked the glass from my hand. It hit the floor with a thud but it didn't break. She shook her head again, tears running down her cheeks.

'I'm sorry,' she said and looked at me. 'I'm sorry. I'm so, so sorry but you need to know – you're not the father.'

I watched her bend to pick up the glass and place it on the coffee table. I watched her take a tea towel from the counter and kneel to mop the floor.

'What do you mean?' I said.

'Wait,' she said. 'Please wait. I really thought you were. I mean, I really hoped you might be.'

I started speaking, started shouting, but everything I said, everything I tried to persuade myself that I was feeling, was a lie. It was only much later, after Carol had passed out on the couch, tear-stained and utterly exhausted, and I stood over her, watching her, that I accepted the truth. What I had felt was not anger but shame; what I had wanted from her was not love but guilt. It rose up inside me with an undeniable clarity: I had known that I was not the baby's father all along.

In the morning, Carol went back to her sister's place. I phoned the department from the couch to cancel my classes, and there I lay, uncertain as to why or how I might get up again.

On the second day, she began to call me hourly. I turned off my phone.

On the third, she sent me messages on Facebook. I stopped checking my account.

She wrote long emails: *I made a mistake* and *I wanted to tell you but you were so happy* and *you made me feel so happy and so safe* and

I was so afraid. I stopped reading them. I deleted them all. I blocked her email address.

Her sister called me.

'Are you fucking serious?' I said.

I wandered from room to room and began to feel a chill, a permanent empty sadness in the apartment. I unboxed the crib and spent an afternoon building it. Once I'd finished, I took a picture and listed it for free on Craigslist. I got four emails in under an hour and deleted them all. I tried to dismantle the crib again but the bolts wouldn't budge. I tore the mattress from its stays and snapped the plywood caging, stuffed the pieces back into the box and dragged the box to the kerb.

I thought about calling my mother but I couldn't bring myself to do it. I emailed her instead and told her what had happened. I waited for a response – and waited. Nothing came.

I called the number that had belonged to my parents when I was a kid. Someone answered, a strange voice but a familiar accent.

'Hello,' I said.

'Hello?' the voice said. 'Hello? Who is this? Are you still there?'

I hung up.

And then I got a call from Dessa Greene wondering if I might be free to fly out for a second round of interviews. I peeled off my sweats and stepped into the shower, turned the water on cold to shock myself into feeling. I shaved and went for a haircut, trawled Expedia for flights. I'd already spent my department travel allowance for the year, so I dipped into the money I'd been putting aside for the baby.

Indiana from the air was a chequerboard of greens and browns. I headed straight from the airport to teach a class of young MAs, who asked intelligent questions and who wanted to hear my answers, and who, long after the class had ended, stayed on talking with me and with a handful of faculty members. Dessa introduced me to her husband, a lanky physicist, and their baby son. The kid had a flat nose and intelligent brown eyes whose gaze I struggled to endure, and then avoided over dinner.

I slept poorly, woke early and went out running. The campus was a small compound of poured concrete surrounded by a copse of trees, beyond which farmland stretched away for miles in all directions. But the library was big and warm: I knew that, if unchecked, I could crawl in there and use up whole years of my life. That afternoon, I attended a brunch hosted by the department chair, a young-eyed old man with hair in his ears and a drooping moustache. It was my job to impress him, though I could hardly bring myself to speak. But as I said my goodbyes and thanked him, he clapped a hand on my shoulder.

'I read an essay of yours somewhere,' he said. 'Some really smart stuff, son. And Dessa thinks the world of you. And I think the world of Dessa.' He leaned close. 'Listen, I probably shouldn't be telling you this until it's gone through the appropriate channels. But I'll want to make you an offer. And what I want, I usually get.'

'Long may that continue,' I said.

'Would you be interested?'

'I would.'

'Good,' he said and thrust into my hand a paper plate of macadamia-nut brownies his wife had baked. 'Best in state.' He winked. 'Take some for the plane.'

I caught a cab to the airport and hustled towards security. The TSA agent squinted at my Irish passport. Yes, I was in the country legally. Yes, I was allowed to work. Sure, here were my visa documents. At length, I made it to the gate. I ordered coffee and sat drinking it and eating the brownies. My phone buzzed, at last, with a call from my mother's number. But when I answered, it was Eamonn.

'Listen,' I said. 'Just put her on the phone.'

'I'm afraid, son,' he said, 'that she can't speak to you right now. She's too upset.'

'*She's* upset? Really, Eamonn, I'm not in the mood.'

'I know the way it is. You've never wanted to know me.'

'Christ,' I said, 'are you serious?'

'But to be honest, I really don't care. I'm not calling you to make friends. Your mother wanted someone to speak with you. And all she has is me.' He paused, and when he resumed his voice seemed somehow to have galvanized. 'See, you forget how long you've been away. You forget it's me who's taken care of her these years. I look after her. And you're her son. So if you need any looking after, well . . .'

I laughed – I couldn't help myself. But soon I felt close to tears. I remembered a morning long ago. The police were downstairs and I was sitting on the ground outside my parents' bedroom calling her name, waiting to be told.

'So, do you want to talk about the thing,' Eamonn said, 'or don't you?'

'I really don't.'

'Where are you?'

'Indiana.'

'What in blazes are you doing there?'

My departure time was nearing. The seats filled up around me. Through the window, beyond the runway, were waves of frosted cornfields.

'To be honest, Eamonn,' I said, 'I really haven't a fucking clue.'

At the first thaw, ploughs pushed the snow into heaps that sat on the corners steaming. I reread the dissertation in preparation for my defence, and as I did I was baffled by the confidence of the voice I heard speaking from its pages. I had expected to feel nervous, but on the morning I just felt embarrassed: of my own work and of myself for having to claim it; but mainly for my supervisor, who had pored over the thing for weeks, teasing it apart and testing it, and who now, unbelievably, pronounced it to be 'excellent'. I batted away his questions easily, dismissed any lingering concerns and promised to address one or two issues in the book manuscript I would soon be under pressure to develop.

Once the formal offer arrived from Indiana, I gave notice to the landlord. I bought boxes for my stuff and set a date with a moving company.

'So, that's it?' Darren said.

This was in his and Emma's apartment the week after spring break. I'd run into Emma at the library and accepted her invitation to a bottle of wine in the evening.

'That's it,' I said.

Emma dandled Sky on her knee and boasted about the traffic on her newly relaunched mommy blog. Darren stroked his cheek and wondered if he should get an MBA. No one mentioned Carol. And as the evening wore on, I foresaw for the three of us a future of dwindling contact. Darren and I would exchange a few jokey emails, invitations for visits that would never come off. Then things would settle down to a card at Christmas and one on Sky's birthday, until inevitably I forgot even about that. On my way to the train, though I wasn't hungry, I stopped at the cruddy noodle joint by the 103rd Street dorms where – sometimes five, six nights a week – I once had eaten dinner before I had anyone to eat with. The broth was a paste of heavy stock, the vegetables limp and pallid. But the taste, as it had been then, was warmth and comfort.

The next day, I collected essays and headed towards my carrel to grade them. On the library steps, I paused a moment by the bronze Alma Mater gazing over the quad. She sat in a throne on a marble plinth with her arms spread out in welcome, her knees pressed together to balance an open book. She held a sceptre in her hand; her head was wreathed in laurels. I watched a squirrel strike a nut against a fold of the statue's gown, and stared up at the building's dome that rose like a hill or an island. I felt at home, as I only ever have done in places I soon would leave. But when my phone rang, I remembered two red balloons printed on a grey sky, held aloft together, chasing a speeding river.

I wasn't Carol's boyfriend, and I wasn't the baby's father, but already as I answered I was racing for the subway, certain that if necessary I could run for miles. I didn't need directions to the hospital.

I knew the way.

Acknowledgements

Thanks are owed to the families Fox, Kelly and Firetog; Gerald Dawe, Deirdre Madden, Mary Morrissy, Brian Lynch and Lilian Foley; all at the Tyrone Guthrie Centre at Annaghmakerrig, Brendan Barrington and Lucy Luck.

I wish gratefully to acknowledge the support of the Arts Council / An Chomhairle Ealaíon.

He just wanted a decent book to read ...

Not too much to ask, is it? It was in 1935 when Allen Lane, Managing Director of Bodley Head Publishers, stood on a platform at Exeter railway station looking for something good to read on his journey back to London. His choice was limited to popular magazines and poor-quality paperbacks – the same choice faced every day by the vast majority of readers, few of whom could afford hardbacks. Lane's disappointment and subsequent anger at the range of books generally available led him to found a company – and change the world.

'We believed in the existence in this country of a vast reading public for intelligent books at a low price, and staked everything on it'
Sir Allen Lane, 1902–1970, founder of Penguin Books

The quality paperback had arrived – and not just in bookshops. Lane was adamant that his Penguins should appear in chain stores and tobacconists, and should cost no more than a packet of cigarettes.

Reading habits (and cigarette prices) have changed since 1935, but Penguin still believes in publishing the best books for everybody to enjoy. We still believe that good design costs no more than bad design, and we still believe that quality books published passionately and responsibly make the world a better place.

So wherever you see the little bird – whether it's on a piece of prize-winning literary fiction or a celebrity autobiography, political tour de force or historical masterpiece, a serial-killer thriller, reference book, world classic or a piece of pure escapism – you can bet that it represents the very best that the genre has to offer.

Whatever you like to read – trust Penguin.